SP/OP

Janet McNeill was born in Dubli[...] minister. She attended school in [...] Classics at St Andrew's University [...] she returned to Ireland and worked as a journalist at the *Belfast Telegraph* until 1933. She married Robert P. Alexander, a senior civil engineer, and they lived in Lisburn while their four children were growing up. Janet began writing plays for radio and then went on to write novels, books for children, short articles and a couple of opera librettos. Some of the children's books have been translated into various languages, including Japanese, and several have been published in the United States.

In 1964 she and her husband moved to England to be nearer their scattered family. Now a widow, she lives in Bristol.

JANET McNEILL

The Maiden Dinosaur

ARLEN HOUSE

THE BLACKSTAFF PRESS

First published in 1964 by Geoffrey Bles
This Blackstaff Press/Arlen House edition is a photolithographic
facsimile of the first edition printed by Cox and Wyman Limited.

First paperback edition published in 1984 by
The Blackstaff Press
3 Galway Park, Dundonald, Belfast BT16 0AN
and
Arlen House, The Women's Press
69 Jones Road, Dublin 3

The purchase of the rights of this work was
assisted by the Author's Royalty Scheme
of the Arts Council/An Chomhairle Ealaíon, Ireland.
The Blackstaff Press gratefully acknowledges the financial assistance
of the Arts Council of Northern Ireland.

Printed in Northern Ireland by
The Universities Press Limited

British Library Cataloguing in Publication Data
McNeill, Janet
The maiden dinosaur
I. Title
823'.914 F   PR6063.A26

ISBN 0 85640 302 4 (Blackstaff)   0 905223 96 9 (Arlen House)

CHAPTER ONE

The door of Helen's flat opened and closed again, and George's familiar step sounded on the stairs. He had made a short stay, although this was Wednesday, early-closing day at Helen's flower shop. Sarah came out of her flat on the floor above in time to follow his progress downstairs, and noticed with interest the blank uninhabited look on his face, and how at the turn of the stairs he halted, pulling his shoulders back and briskly re-arranging the well-known features that persisted in looking so young, as if his thick white hair were a joke. She admired the drill, and wondered if it made any difference to his state of mind. He swung out across the hall, as conscious of his performance as he would have been if he had known she was watching, and touched the flower in his buttonhole encouragingly before he disappeared.

After she had heard his car driving off she knocked on Helen's door with gentle deliberate pleasure. It was appropriate that what had in Sarah's childhood been the solemn acres of Mama's bedroom was now part of Helen's flat, since both in their way were Holy Ground.

There was no answer, but she had seen Helen's car in the garage when she had returned from afternoon school. "I'll call for you in half an hour," she said, opening the door sufficiently to make sure that Helen heard her.

Still no reply. Helen's silence, the drawn blinds – though the white March light had not yet begun to fade – and the shaded lamp beside the bed were significant and reproachful. Sarah felt rebuked, as she was meant to. But Helen's calendar was crowded with festivals of remembrance and little private celebrations of sorrow, and it was easy to make a mistake.

What was it this time? Was this the anniversary of her

7

wedding day – all of them bridesmaids, masses of organdie and brigades of top hats and 'Oh Perfect Love', the whole nuptial lot – or was this the day that Oliver whom Helen really loved had been shot down over Germany, or the day her nine-year-old daughter fell off her bicycle under the wheels of a lorry on the way to school, or the child's birthday perhaps, or the day three years after she was killed when Hubert walked out of the house and never came back? There was plenty to choose from. Sarah was filled with impatience and shame and pity.

"I'm so sorry." She stood at the door unable to go farther or to find an excuse for leaving.

"That's all right." Helen was prostrate on the bed.

"Is there anything I can do?"

"No. No, really."

Helen's hand clutching a handkerchief was raised from the counterpane and laid down again, dismissing the possibility of help. "Do? What can you do?" It was hard to forgive Helen her dramatics much as one loved her. There was something about Helen that would make her unique among a boat-load of shades crossing the Styx in the rush hour. Even at school the sight of her leapt out across a hockey pitch or class-room.

"What are you staring at, Sarah Vincent? Don't you know it's rude to stare?"

"Yes, Helen."

Then Helen would laugh, throwing back her long coil of corn-coloured hair and adjusting the ribbon bow that perched on it like a blackbird. Sometimes as a special favour Sarah was allowed to brush Helen's hair, when it had become tangled after games.

"Who's rude, then?"

"I am, Helen."

"Did you hear that, Rose? Sarah Vincent says she's rude!"

And they linked arms, laughing, the constant pair, Rose and Helen.

"Did you finish that French exercise?"

8

"Oh yes, Helen."

"Pass it over."

And Sarah passed it.

"A good thing someone's got brains."

Brains were no help now. "There must be something I can do," Sarah persisted unhappily.

"There isn't, really," Helen assured the ceiling.

Brains at least told her that Helen was over the worst, whatever it had been, and Sarah sighed heavily and shut the door, thinking before her fingers released the Victorian door-knob how often her father's hand had closed the same door after much the same conversation. She had watched from the landing above, trying to hear what was said, blaming herself for not feeling more sorry for Mama who was ill, and blaming Papa because there seemed a softness in the way he accepted defeat. Was it a virtue in him, or was it a kind of cunning stupidity? And was it worse to be fourteen and not know any of the answers, or fifty-two and know them all and that they were inconclusive?

She returned to her own room and the stack of Latin exercises. Caesar was in an indecisive frame of mind. No more straightforward throwing of bridges or striking of camps. He had paused to consider the object of the exercise and 'wondered whether' or 'thought that surely' and it was obvious that the Lower Fourth did not share his mood. Sarah's green biro was by turns exclamatory, sorrowful and indignant, and the exercise books were embellished with her comments in the small, wholly legible handwriting that was so inappropriate to her physical shape and style.

This room, now her study in the second-floor flat which she had retained for herself, had been the sewing-room of the house where she was born, Thronehill, a monument to middle-class Victorian prosperity, on the north side of Belfast Lough. In her girlhood this room was the territory of Mrs. McLennon who came to sew on Thursdays. Mrs McLennon was a neatly-upholstered and emphatic little woman whose

9

mouth was puckered perpetually by pins. She took them out to eat the meals that Ellen brought on a tray and put them back again when she had wiped her mouth. Then the see-sawing foot set the machine chasing again across the cloth.

Sarah sat at the window, large, plain and untidy, and sometimes the green biro rested a moment as she stared into the garden. A pair of seagulls that had come in from the Lough invaded the lawn with a bold disturbance of wings and rose again over the high trees behind the shrubbery. The girl who lived in the servants' flat over the stable – Florence's girl, Felicity – was hanging a row of undergarments on a line she had rigged up in the old greenhouse where Papa's cinerarias used to blaze. Sarah watched her with affectionate interest. The garments were as bright as the cinerarias used to be, though less substantial. After them a string of nappies, steaming gently. Oh, poor Papa!

Someone knocked.

"Come in."

It was Felicity's husband who resembled Pan and whose name was Justin. Where were the Roberts nowadays, the Williams, the Henrys, the Charleses? Justin had large fringed eyes and a long nose, and his hair was like a cap of fur cut to the shape of his head and glued on.

"Am I interrupting you or something?"

"No, of course not." This version of male beauty was intriguing.

"Felicity said you'd be busy." He leant, graceful and relaxed, in the doorway, like someone making a stage entrance. Any moment now he will break into a *pas seul* or strike an attitude to deliver an aria. "Felicity says you are the devil for work. She admires you very much."

"Really? And what does she want?"

"Actually it's me – I'm cooking. You don't have any saffron, do you?"

"It is I – haven't got," she corrected. "Saffron? No."

"Pity, I said you would have. I thought all you ladies had terrific store cupboards and were fabulous cooks."

"You flatter me. I'm older than that, the last of the original Ladies. Women of my generation either learned the domestic arts or were educated. I was educated."

"Oh yes, I know." His tone expressed respect.

"We had Clara to cook for us."

"Clara – how superb!"

"So was her cooking. She and Ellen slept in the room over the stables where you are now."

"Clara and Ellen! *Papier poudré* and feather boas and prayer-books and curling irons and stay-laces and chamber-pots."

They laughed. She liked this boy-husband of Felicity's. She forgave him his flippancy for his narcissistic flamboyance and knew he overlooked her dowdiness out of respect for her intelligence.

"And Rosaries and bleeding hearts," she added. "How that intrigued me! I envied them on Sundays coming home from early Mass to serve breakfast with a newly done-over soul. I had to wait until eleven to take my Presbyterian conscience to Church to wrestle with it."

"Did you wrestle with it much?"

"It was all rather negative. We were instructed to be pure, but no one gave us any information how to be anything else. Why are you cooking for Felicity?"

"The baby." He was still uneasy about fatherhood.

"What do you use saffron for, anyway?"

He widened his improbable eyes. "My dear, you must know."

"I can boil an egg and I can open tins. None of the men in my life could do either. It would have shocked me deeply if they could."

"You're making it up," he accused.

"No, indeed. The Irishman was always clever at withstanding domestication, especially up here in the North."

"Slow to learn?"

"Not at all. The Scot in us. Can you imagine John Knox drying dishes?"

"I don't know that I can even imagine John Knox."

"You should try," she scolded, squinting over her glasses at him. "Now run away and make your messes. I'm going out and I want to finish these exercises. Sorry about the – what was it? – saffron."

"Not to worry."

She chewed over the possible Classical justification for this construction. The boy turned in the doorway.

"I say. You mustn't mind me – I may be wildly off the rails again – but you can't do the Charleston, can you?"

She slapped the exercise book shut. "And the Indian Rope Trick," she assured him.

"No, but – can you? I'm not sure of my dates, but I thought —"

"Actually," she said, "I can."

"Marvellous. Oh, wonderful woman. Please come on!"

The exercise books slid and tumbled as he pulled her up. She enjoyed the touch of his hands and her closeness to him.

"Come on! A demonstration. The original Charleston."

"It will be very bad for my bad leg," she warned.

"But very good for Felicity and me," he said, narrowing his eyes to smile.

He pushed back a chair and with the delicate skill of an elephant Sarah danced the Charleston. Her knees bent, her feet slid, she performed unsuspected agilities. Back and forward, side to side, exact and predictable, like a piece of good Latin prose.

"'If he's just a clever – Lover he will never – Do – Hoo – Hoo.'" she sang breathily, and Justin said, "I should think not." He clapped his applause, maintaining the beat, and then fell in at her side, imitating.

"Enough, enough!" She stopped, gasping and seized the

back of a chair to steady herself. "I haven't done that for thirty years."

"Did you dance a lot?"

"I enjoyed dancing," she said, side-tracking.

"I've got it! Look – I've got it!" He charlestoned concentratedly. "That's right, isn't it?" He broke off long enough to kiss her cheek and picking up the rhythm again danced to the door, which he opened, still dancing. Neither of them expected the fourteen-year-old schoolgirl who stood on the landing clutching her text books.

"Sally!"

"Good afternoon, Miss Vincent."

Sally was already blushing rosily. Every now and again, rarely and more rarely, there was a girl in the Lower School who trembled and coloured when Sarah spoke to her, who squirmed deliciously in her seat while Sarah discussed her essay, and was discovered often outside the Staff Room door at the time Sarah left it in the afternoon.

"Oh, Sally – didn't I tell you I couldn't take you for your special tuition this afternoon?"

"No, Miss Vincent."

"My dear" – the girl grew rosier – "I am sorry. I thought I had told you. But I have to go out."

"It's quite all right, Miss Vincent – really." Her eyes came round to Justin who was smiling at her.

"This is Justin Robins – Sally Clark."

"Hi, Sally."

"Hallo."

"Come to the class-room after prayers tomorrow, Sally. We'll fix up then when I can take you. Now off you go, both of you."

She made shoo-ing movements with her hands. Justin offered his arm with a flourish. The girl giggled as she accepted it, and he led her away.

Sarah closed the door behind them. She would be late now for the meeting. They met on the afternoon of the third Wednesday

13

of every month. She looked forward to it with pleasure, and at the last moment was attacked by misgivings. When authority is part of your daily stock-in-trade, personal friendships require a good deal of adjustment. The meeting meant that she would have to take off her armour and she wasn't sure whether the atmosphere would prove warm enough for the soft body underneath. It would be warm enough, it always was. But now, as if on the edge of a springboard, trying to prepare herself for surrender, her heart protested that she wasn't ready and her mind suspected that there was something comic about this gathering of middle-aged schoolfriends.

She made her preparations hastily and with purposeful carelessness, in case it might appear that she had any hope of improving her appearance. This seemed more honest and less effort, and it saved time. No one will be able to say, "Poor old Sarah, how hard she tries." She came out of her room on to the silent landing, inhabited still by the solid pieces of furniture that had peopled it in her childhood. Although the house was divided now into flats she had left the core of it unchanged, partly because she knew herself to be a woman without taste and had no confidence in making changes, and partly because the heavy pictures and the mahogany offered a memorial more convincingly positive than her own heart could always provide.

Mama, thirty-four years dead, stirred on her sofa in the drawing-room. Sarah heard the light insistent cough, the tinkling cow-bell lifted and laid again. Mama had various voices. Sometimes she spoke as childhood's ear remembered, sometimes through the schoolgirl caricature with which Sarah had fought maternal domination, rarely as the adult who demanded terrified pity. The drawing-room was part of Addie's flat now, but when there was no sound from it it was impossible to deny that on the other side of the door lay anything other than the pattern of chairs, occasional tables, mirrors, ornaments, tasselled curtains that had furnished the setting for her mother's sofa.

"Where are you going, dear?"

"To tea with the girls, Mama."

"What are you wearing? When will you be back? Tell Rose to give her mother my dear love."

It had pleased Mama when Rose's mother died two years before she did, and it was twenty-seven years now since Rose's death.

"I will, I will."

"And if your Papa is in the conservatory —" But the clock on the landing struck and Mama's voice was lost.

Tobacco in the hall, and with it the sense of irritation at her adored Father's anxious goodwill.

"Good-bye, Papa."

"Going out? Where are you off to this time?"

Papa attempted to flatter her by fostering the myth that her social life was a busy one. He probably expected in return her support for the theory that his work at the office was arduous. He had been a Solicitor, occupied sometimes in the leisurely business of conveyancing, and sometimes in other ways, all of them pleasant. Her childhood was littered by Papa's enthusiasms: the health exercises, the operatic singing classes, the aviary, the badminton court. They burnt themselves out, or, if they were expensive, were extinguished when there was no more of Mama's money available for them.

"Off to tea with the girls, Papa."

"Ha! Another tea-party! 'The tongue can no man tame!'" His forefinger caressed the bridge of his nose, then came closer and tilted her chin towards him. She had not seen Papa's face so clearly for some time, that handsome paternal mask he maintained for her. His eyes – too blue for a man – searched hers for some reflection of himself.

Sarah felt again the keen grief she had experienced when he died and the regret that the mask had never been wholly removed.

"Enjoy yourself," he said. "All right for money, are you?" Reluctantly his hand moved towards his pocket.

She said, "Mama gave me some," and tried not to notice how his face lightened and how quickly the hand came away.

From the breakfast-room came the sound of the piano – Miss Fennimore propelling herself through Beethoven's Minuet in G. Papa heard it and turned at once, pressing Sarah's fingers to speed the farewell. The door of the breakfast-room opened and Sarah heard the music stop abruptly before she left the house for her tea-party.

Belfast's streets were crowded by the first wave of home-going office workers. The City Hall, self-important in daylight, now looked like the backcloth for a Ruritanian romance. Lights shone from the windows and the shrill murmuration of thousands of homing starlings shredded the air. The sky was luminous, palely blue.

The table at the window was waiting for them in the café across the street. It was reserved, every third Wednesday. Once Sarah had overheard one of the waitresses describing their party to another waitress. "The usual old plate of cakes at the window." Sarah was amused but she didn't tell the others. It wouldn't have amused them, since they tried more than she did.

'Sarah makes no effort.' She might have written it with justice on her own report. That was the line Miss Fennimore used to take when Mama was lying down with the blinds drawn after lunch and Papa had returned to his office. Miss Fennimore was fond of the Elder Sister approach. "You ought to do more about yourself, Sarah. You could look so much nicer. You don't mind me saying this, do you, dear? You have such good eyes. No, I wouldn't say it if I didn't mean it. I wish you'd let me help you – I'd like to, really. I wish I had eyes like yours." And she dropped her thick white lids quickly. She had small colourless eyes, redeemed by red-gold lashes, and the lids were heavy, moist and faintly veined with blue. Miss Fennimore had come to live at Thronehill when illness immobilised Mama. She was the daughter of a distant relative, an active and girlish thirty-eight, in whom light-heartedness seemed a useful habit.

Mama – in the voice in which Sarah imitated her – chipped in: "Sarah, is your hat straight? Have you your handkerchief? Remember to ask where to go if you want to. And sit up, cross your ankles and keep your knees together."

"I will, I will."

'Sarah makes no effort.' This had been policy rather than negligence. "I suppose it's the uniform they make them wear," Papa used to say, looking at his daughter with a puzzled kind of pity and rubbing his nose, "is it specially designed to make them look like that?"

She knew that this pity turned to shame when she left school and graduated into the silk dresses and cloth coats Mama planned for her and over which Mrs. McLennon laboured. "Such a lovely quality of cloth." Mrs. McLennon's hand passed over it lovingly. Did she feel beneath it Sarah's shrinking flesh? Was it a sin to turn your face away so that you didn't breathe Mrs. McLennon's breath? But even the cloth's excellence didn't better the result. They were mutually ashamed, Papa and Sarah. Sometimes the shame strengthened the love between them, but sometimes she knew that he became angry at her thick ankles in shiny silk stockings – stockings that did not hide the dark hair now evident below them – the sad cloche hats, her dull complexion and the figure that burgeoned solidly beneath her clothes. "Who *is* she like?" puzzled relatives asked. "Love me more because I am plain," Sarah's eyes entreated her father, "love me more because I need it."

She regretted now that she had not made some effort to meet the afternoon's occasion. She might have tried. The porridge-coloured coat with raglan sleeves and the velvet tam (the texture and colour of lichen) were garments in which she felt at home. The gloves, her only impulse to finery, were an obvious mistake. Unsubstantial and frivolous in transparent nylon, they were stretched tightly over her large hands, making them look like those of a female impersonator.

'CROSS NOW' Street lamps jerked on, killing all the remaining light in the sky. Instead of obeying the sign she drew back on to the steps of the Insurance Office, fidgeting with her handbag, her gloves, her umbrella, the library books she had hoped to change. Inside the class-room inanimate objects were her servants, outside it she was their fool. Someone came out from the office and jostled her so that she dropped her newspaper and heard herself say "I'm sorry," unnecessarily, since the fault was his. On an impulse she set down her books and poked at her hair, then rummaged in her handbag for the little phial of perfume that years ago had come her way from a Christmas tree – an unsuitable gift for which she had felt unreasonably grateful. It had never been opened before, but with some effort the stopper yielded and she sprinkled the liquid on her fingers and carried it to her temples. It was sweet, clinging, full of flowers, an amber scent of amorous perfume.

Sarah liked perfume though she did not wear it. Her upbringing had never encouraged her to think that the human body required to have any perfumes added to it, or any taken away. Unfortunate odours were in the category of hair on legs and dark stains in the armpits of tussore blouses. One ignored them, they no longer existed. '*Honi soit qui mal y pongs*', as Addie had put it in the Junior Cloakroom, forty years ago. There had been a little tut-tutting about Addie being at school, since her father was in trade. But here in the darkened doorway Sarah breathed the scent deeply, allowing her senses to expand and swoon. Silken voluptuous couches. Her umbrella slid and clattered to the ground.

It was when she had screwed the bottle tight, clicked her handbag shut and bent to retrieve her umbrella that she realised she had forgotten to take off her gloves. She pulled them off, scent-sodden, and put them in her pocket, irritated at her feminine inadequacy. Another figure left the office

18

behind her and as he passed she heard him sniff speculatively and she giggled in appalled appreciation of herself, lurking in a doorway, smelling like a pick-up.

'CROSS NOW' again. But she still needed some vestige of self-esteem to propel her, late, gloveless and apologetic, into the middle of the tea-party. Perhaps someone might have noticed her verses in the magazine. They would not have exploded with a golden fanfare for them as they had for her, but perhaps someone had seen them. Or would they? The verses were scholarly, the magazine thin and intellectual. But perhaps, when the inquiries for each others' families were discharged – that excursion into adult territory they permitted each other – the verses might be mentioned. Sarah was the clever one. The pride that lived in her like an animal, the pride that did terrible things to her, would surely earn a tit-bit. She had taught herself to hide the beast's existence from others, but found that he behaved better if she acknowledged him to herself, and if he were fed she could hold her own at the tea-party.

'CROSS NOW'. She was stepping out when two of the girls from school came up the pavement and she stepped back just in time. Betty Marks, like a Victorian portrait, full stolid face terminating unexpectedly in a delicate chin, eyes slightly prominent and her hair parted in the middle and looped serenely – she was going to fail her O Level English if her religious fervour didn't cool off, her essays read like tracts this term – and Jane Best, last summer's delicious barefoot Titania, who had got her photograph in all the papers and spread verrucca disastrously through the Upper School just before the Tennis Championships. This wasn't the way they walked through the school corridors, nor had they learned in school to use their eyes like that. The lighted shop windows shone on their silky faces; they were beautiful, with the undefinable alien beauty which Sarah noticed in her girls when she met them outside the class-room, and which alarmed her because they seemed creatures from another planet.

She held her breath as Betty and Jane crossed within feet of her. Surely the fall-out of perfume could hardly escape them; from anxiety and suppressed laughter she must be exuding a thousand blossoms per second. But heads together, chattering, they went by without turning, the lights said 'CROSS NOW' again, and this time she obeyed them.

CHAPTER TWO

"THE Ladies are up above," the waitress said, suspending operations with her nail file as she jerked her head in the direction of the stairs.

Sarah was conscious of her contemplative eye as she ascended, and knew that her glance drew those of the people at other tables to her stiffly ascending back, her legs in elastic stockings and her unfashionable shoes. She didn't want pity or object to criticism (since she knew it was justified), but she would have liked them to think that if the choice had been hers her legs would have been like the pearly dimpled pair, touchingly innocent of seams, of the girl in high heels who overtook and passed her. She would have liked them to think this, though it wasn't strictly true.

There they were: Mary, Joyce, Enid, Addie. Addie must have come straight from school. Florence hadn't arrived yet.

"Oh dear, am I late?" On the brink of identification she rebelled against it.

"I think an order mark would be in order, Sarah Vincent," Addie said plummy-mouthed, in imitation of Miss Hodgkiss, vintage Lower Fifth, 1922; Miss Hodgkiss, long-nosed, austere and pale except for the red triangle of skin which lay, winter or summer, in the opening of her blouse.

Their laughter reached out like tentacles, wrapped itself round her and drew her in.

"Where's Helen?"

"She couldn't come," Sarah said, adding untruthfully, "she sent her love." They raised their eyebrows registering varying interpretations.

Here was Florence, peeling her gloves from her ringed

fingers. The aura of fashionable committee meetings hung about her, as it always did, but even Florence showed a trace of anxiety – her forehead twitched below its floral turban.

"Sorry, my dears, but the meeting went on and on – you know how these things do! Everyone's pet hobby horse and a Chairman who simply hadn't a clue."

"Hallo, Florence." Addie lit her cigarette. "That was a frightful picture of you in the paper last week. How did you have the nerve to wear a hat like that? We killed ourselves over it."

They agreed with affectionate malice; they had all killed themselves.

Florence wasn't prepared to give in at once. She smiled, spreading her hands prettily. "My dears, did you see it? We did quite fantastically well. Such nice people and a wildly good cause. Really you've no idea how much suffering there is – I mean if people only *knew*. Three hundred and sixty-four we made."

"Was it a new fur coat?"

"New? Of course not. But people expect you to dress up a little. They'd feel insulted if you didn't."

Florence's tone had become apologetic, she was weakening. She had been something of a nonentity at school, nowhere near the Rose-Helen status. They had been surprised at her emergence and success as a public figure in the city since her marriage. It was out of character, and they felt a need to deflate her before she was accepted.

"It must be very expensive, opening those Sales and things," Mary commented, "or are you one of the Personalities who so graciously consents to do it for a handsome fee?"

"No such luck." Florence blinked her lashes quickly, the way they remembered her blinking in class, and her cheeks grew pinkly mottled through her make-up. "It's terribly expensive, actually – you've no idea."

22

This contented them, and they let her in.

"I thought the hat was rather nice."

It was unusual of Joyce to express an independent opinion. Joyce was the youngest of them, just around forty. She was Rose's baby sister. Sometimes Rose used to bring her along to parties because there was no one at home to play with, and they gave her their outworn dolls and petted her, and she played quietly. A neat biddable child. They felt responsibility for her when Rose died and invited her to the tea-parties and petted her again. It was the same motive, they believed, that prompted Maurice to marry her when a decent interval had elapsed. A Deceased Wife's Sister was permissible now. They turned out in force to the wedding. It was their memorial to Rose, and no one doubted that it was Maurice's memorial too.

Addie was talking about the German girl who had stayed with them last summer. Addie was the Twitterer, unfailingly jaunty and unfortunate, with an elderly ailing husband. Gerald had retired now, but Addie still kept her job as Lady Cook at school, cycling at full speed between her work and the ground-floor flat which they occupied in Thronehill. "A very nice girl, from Bremen. The idea was that she would help me, but I spent most of the time running round after her, and you've no idea how bad she was for poor Gerald's blood pressure. Talk about cleavage – coming or going, I don't know which was worse!"

There was a little unwilling laughter and they sat more firmly on their chairs. Addie really shouldn't go on like that. She was always apt to overdo the frankness. "Nothing to look forward to," she had declared some years back, "nothing left to look forward to except Change of Life."

They hadn't looked forward to it, nor were they enjoying it, and those who had accomplished it felt aggrieved that it left them feeling so much the same as they had before. What had they expected? A certain pleasurable immunity, a seat in

23

the stalls, perhaps, a kind of stability to match their older faces; they had not found them.

Addie had obtained a medical book on the attendant hazards. "So many variations to choose from one can hardly go wrong. The chief thing is to keep the mind interested." They had kept their minds interested.

"This *Fräulein*," Addie told them, "she read *Jane Eyre* in bed, and every morning she used to retail the latest instalment at breakfast; the suspense was terrible."

They laughed, noticing that Addie had had something done to her teeth, and trying to make an unobtrusive analysis. One after another they had all had something done to their teeth, smiling bravely and unfamiliarly and avoiding coconut at the next tea-party. No one liked the innovations, they offended them in the way that a child is offended by the loss of something familiar. But after a while the changes were forgotten, as if their present appearances were only symbols, cues to the images of girlhood that memory retained.

Together with her new teeth Addie was wearing the lavish assembly of colours and ornaments that they expected of her. A magpie might have chosen to dress like this. A pink hat with feather trimming, blue-flowered scarf, pearly spider pin, green coat, two gold mice on the lapel, giving her the overall appearance of an animated Christmas tree. If there were any domestic decoration for gallantry Addie deserved it. There would just have been room for it between the two mice.

"How is Kitty?" asked Enid.

Kitty, who was George's wife, was one of their casualties. The tea-party took on a minor key.

"I haven't been for ages," Mary said, and speared a crumpet. The melted butter welled up in beads as she pressed it. "Ever so often I mean to go, but to tell you the truth that sort of thing gives me the creeps; if there was anything one felt one could do —"

Mary was plump, comely, occasionally skittish. She had a highly successful conspiracy with life to ignore its more unpleasant realities. She had reared baby after baby with steam-roller placidity and was now a grandmother. Amiably cunning, she by-passed anything that would shock or hurt. "There isn't really anything one can do for depressives. Of course one is desperately sorry – who wouldn't be? – but nobody can really help them except themselves. At least they keep them pretty well doped-up, don't they? It's kinder, I suppose." Her teeth closed on crumpet.

Joyce asked, "Is she as bad as ever?" From a neat little girl Joyce had grown into a pretty woman whose prettiness surprised you every time you met her because you had forgotten about it in between. It was significantly some time after Rose's death before anybody had thought of comparing her with her beautiful sister.

"She's getting worse every time I see her." Sarah was angry with Mary.

"Is she still at home?"

"Oh yes."

"I wonder if she wouldn't be better away," Mary said. "Some of those places are wonderful, they say. And there's not the same chance for them to play for sympathy."

Sarah snorted, but didn't trust herself to speak.

"Do you see Kitty often, Sarah?" Florence's query was sharp, since good works were her province. "You are weird, Sarah, some of the things you do."

Sometimes they were weird. It was a game that Sarah indulged in sporadically. She was a little ashamed of it. Sometimes loving Helen wasn't enough, especially since she knew her love was a burden. If Helen were cold or difficult or deliberately tiresome it was easy to lift the telephone and ring up someone – anyone – who would play her game. "It's been simply ages, you know how time goes on, goodness knows what one does with it. I've often wondered about you. Couldn't we meet sometime?" The warmth in her voice almost convinced her and she made sure that the person at the other end was one who would be willing to be convinced. After that a lunch date, a reminiscence, and a *sorti* into intimacy that lasted long enough to see lunch through and was all the more cordial because both of them knew it would lead to a six-months' silence and a Christmas card. And yet there was always the niggling hope that there might be something more, some rare exchange of sympathy or emotion. "My gracious," Helen would say, flicking critically through the cards on Sarah's mantelpiece in December, "what possesses you to keep up with *her*?"

No one remembered that they had liked Kitty very much at school. Her image was dim and vaguely unappealing. It was only because of her illness that they were reminded of her now.

"I never knew she was religious; she certainly never showed much sign of it."

"Is that her line now? Well, that's one of the ways we can go," Addie contributed knowledgeably, "quite common, really."

"Yes, but Kitty! You remember the time the money was missing from the lunch-box. I didn't say anything, but I always thought it was Kitty."

Florence smoothed out her expensive gloves and said, "Surely if anybody's religiously-minded it ought to be a great help to them when they're ill; but if she's really psychotic —"

Sarah's cheeks tightened and flushed. "She is really very unhappy and it doesn't help her what sort of a name you put to it."

There was a brief embarrassed pause. This wasn't the time or the place. Sarah had said too much. But their embarrassment annoyed Sarah and her contralto voice rose strongly, "And as for saying that she's gone religious —"

They glanced at each other uneasily. Then Florence said adroitly, "Basingstoke, my dear," and they were glad of the

excuse to laugh. What a marvellous M
made thirty odd years ago!

Sarah too was faintly relieved, a
extricating her from too much emo

"More tea, anyone?" Mary raised
Florence – Addie – Enid?"

Florence passed her cup. Enid sa
George; especially a man so mucl

They agreed, but tepidly. In th
were cardboard. What had Georg
like that? He must have done something.

"You'd never guess from his voice what he had to go home
to," Joyce said. George's voice was heard on broadcasts two
or three times a week.

Florence accepted her refilled cup but refused cakes, thinking inaudibly but so obviously of her hips that the other ladies
were reminded of their own.

Enid began a racy account of what she called her private
madhouse. She kept house for her father and two elderly
uncles, incredible old gentlemen in their nineties, gentle and
jolly, mildly dotty; every week they chartered a taxi to take
them to a séance where they contacted their three brothers
and six sisters who had crossed to the other side before them.
They listened gratefully, tidying Kitty away at the backs of
their minds.

"I saw your poem, Sarah," Addie said unexpectedly.

The beast woke up and purred. Sarah's pleasure, coming on the heels of her indignation about Kitty, made her
weak.

"Did you? My verses?" The correction had no significance
except to herself, but she needed to make it.

"Another poem! You didn't tell us."

"You are clever, Sarah." Joyce opened her pretty eyes
widely. She had adored Sarah since she was a junior and
Sarah a prefect. Sarah was now a plain untidy old woman,
but there was still something.

always the brainy one."

ster used to say 'Sarah Vincent has real talent.'
ars, do you remember how passionately we loved
rester?"

y laughed indulgently. Miss Forrester reading Tenny-
or 'The Listeners', her hair mildly fluffy from the tongs,
er Liberty blouse, the way she stood beside the open window
with her lisle-stockinged legs set apart, one hand at her
swinging necklace.

'How the silence surged softly backward
And the plunging hoofs were gone.'

Miss Forrester's eyes, large and slightly prominent, were
lifted from the page, confronting her class with a kind of
challenge, and through each blue-serged breast ran a tremor
of ecstasy – ecstasy which adult relationships had sometimes
disappointingly not rivalled.

"I'm dying to read it, Sarah. You haven't got it with you, I
suppose."

"No," she lied, while the beast preened himself.

"Most of the modern poetry is so queer, but I'm sure I
could understand yours."

The beast lay down and sulked.

But Sarah was grateful to Addie. She respected Addie's
agile mind. Probably Addie guessed about the beast, perhaps
she remembered how he had strutted at school when
Sarah's essays were read aloud in class. It was possible that
Addie had a private, lesser beast of her own, for she wrote
pedestrian and slick little articles that sometimes appeared in
the local papers, and was herself secretary of one of the literary
societies in the city.

She watched Florence leaning back in her chair. It was odd
to realise that the other people in the restaurant who looked
at Florence would only see a smart middle-aged woman, but
Sarah saw Sabrina, Sabrina of the Lower Fifth, the summer
they did *Comus* out in the school garden on the headmistress's

28

lawn backed by shrubberies and with the bicycle shed swathed in painted sacking: Sabrina, in blue-green draperies, her ringlets lying loose on her shoulders, Sabrina entering from the sooty laurels seated in a bath-chair transformed into a marine chariot by the huge cardboard shells they had painted in the Art Class and stuck on with glue.

> 'Sabrina fair
> Listen where thou art sitting
> Under the grassy-green translucent wave.'

Florence gracefully relaxes as her nymphs propel her over the grass, her eyes translucent, mouth parted, the butter-muslin yielding to the airs of the June afternoon, her hair lifting as if by sea-breezes. Sarah remembered it momentarily as the true and single eye of childhood had seen it, without any gloss of nostalgia or amusement.

"You're not listening, Sarah." Mary was holding out to her the teacup she had refilled. "You're miles away."

"I was remembering Sabrina and all that caper."

They rocked with laughter, teacups and cakes suspended.

"Sabrina! How funny it was! That bath-chair! And how the shells wobbled! And our suspenders flapped against our legs and Miss Forrester told us to tuck them in. And when it rained! The Bishop was there – do you remember? And the gardener's dog got loose, and – oh dear, oh dear!"

Other tables were noticing them, and they recovered their poise at once, a little shamefaced.

"We'd have thought this tea-party just as funny then if we could have seen ourselves," Addie said, handing cakes.

"I suppose we would."

They looked round at each other and mocked their middle-age critically and gently.

"Mary – all that cream!"

"I know, I know." Her lips folded it in.

They discussed waistlines and diets, touching briskly on constipation.

29

Someone remembered the Greek Class, and how Sarah was always the one picked on to translate the sexy bits.

"I think Mr. Allen fastened on Sarah so that he wouldn't have to do it himself. He knew she was the only one of us who could."

"Not at all. He was a wicked old man and he enjoyed watching her. 'The sweet shames of the marriage bed!' Oh, Sarah, it was always you!"

From their experience of marriage beds they smiled at her inexperience and thought it was funny that she was the one Mr. Allen had picked.

"Do you suppose the papers are right about Teenagers?" Mary ruffled her forehead. "I mean – are they really like that?"

Sometimes they discussed Sex – the public image of it that was now surprisingly an admissible topic of conversation. Occasionally on a sudden impulse two of them might attempt a personal confidence on the subject, but this rarely led anywhere since each soon suspected that they weren't talking about the same thing.

"Are they really like it says in the papers?"

"Sarah would know. They're her business."

"Sarah, is it true? Even while they're at school, it says. Sixty per cent of the girls in the senior classes."

"Is it true, Sarah?"

"I don't know," she said unwillingly.

"Surely – by looking at them —"

No. She resented their curiosity and wanted fiercely to defend the girls she loved but didn't understand. She felt there should be something on their faces that would tell her if what the papers said was true. They were beautiful girls. Perhaps it was her fault that she didn't know.

"My dears, what innocents we were!" Addie lit another cigarette. They discussed their innocence, thread by thread, and the stages of the fabric's collapse.

Sarah said nothing. She was walking along the empty

sunlit stretch of road again, smelling the sharp smell from hot privet hedges. The man was there. She saw his eyes and the way he smiled. The smile held her attention before she saw what he was doing. She couldn't look away. Unable for a frozen moment even to move she broke loose at last from her terror and ran home, her schoolbag banging between her shoulders. Papa and Mama were in the garden. "My dear – Sarah – what has happened?" She tried to tell them, but again she saw his face. There were no words to tell with. "Come on, dear – what was it!" "I saw a man —" They seemed to understand. "He didn't touch you, did he?" "Touch me?" Leprosy? And yet not leprosy. Even at the time, through her shocked distress she thought it peculiar that they didn't ask anything else. "You're sure he didn't touch you, dear?" Whatever it was they knew about it.

Papa was bedding out snapdragon plants. He told her to hold her hands out and gave her some seedlings. "Come and help me, dear." Dutifully, keeping her eyes wide open, she set each plant in the soil. They are doing this to help me. It doesn't help me, but they are kind. Or is this their fault in some way, and are they ashamed?

A couple of months ago she had attended a Juvenile Court with four of her pupils. A youth was charged. The girls were called to give evidence.

"Was this the man you saw beside the gate into the park."

"Yes."

"You're quite sure about that?"

Yes, they were sure.

"Did you notice anything unusual about him?"

They had noticed something.

"Will you tell his Worship what you noticed?"

They told him.

"Did he say anything to you?"

"Yes."

"Will you tell the Court what he said."

They repeated the words the man had used, softly but clearly. "He asked, 'Did you like what you saw?'" Their hair lay back like aureoles under the school berets and their foreheads were gentle and untroubled.

"You are sure that is what he said?"

Oh yes, they were quite sure.

Afterwards on the way back to school they chattered complainingly about an essay they had to write on Wordsworth, ecstatically about a new kind of filling in a chocolate bar, appreciatively about one of the policemen who was like a policeman in a television series. One of them intended to wash her hair that evening. Another promised to set it. Monsters or innocents? Sarah didn't know.

"You're not listening, Sarah."

Addie was off about the German girl again.

"I'm sorry," Sarah said.

But the tea-party had in any case passed its peak. The jollity had gone on long enough, now it creaked. They were all restive, remembering that it often ended like this, a tiresome anticlimax to the instinct of affection that had prompted them to come, affection bred in nurseries and schoolrooms, by their parents' acquaintance with each others' parents, by the habits of life and thought surviving, as snow survives, in this provincial Northern city. All they had achieved was schoolgirl heartiness, trivialities, cloakroom chatter. Looking for sincerity they had contented themselves with caricature, in which there seemed for them a special kind of safety.

Florence stroked her gloves again. "I must go, we're dining out."

Enid consulted her watch. "My dears, is it really as late as that? All those old madmen of mine —"

Addie's German girl was a bore, so was Addie. None of them was listening. They remembered excuses why they must break the party up.

32

"Just a minute. I've got news for you. I've been meaning to tell you, but I didn't know how." It was Joyce.

"What is it, Joyce?"

There *was* something different about Joyce this afternoon. She looked excited, nervous and yet with an air of importance. She wasn't behaving like Rose's little sister. They sat down again, impatiently indulgent.

"Come on, Joyce."

To their complete amazement Joyce blushed. The colour spread across her small indefinite features into the softness of her hair. She looked round them, and then down at her hands.

"I told Maurice I was going to tell you. I knew you'd be surprised."

They looked at her in silent inquiry and she nodded, smiling, with her lips closed.

Astonishment and mental mathematics silenced them.

"Well?" Joyce sounded challenging, almost bold. "Surely someone's going to say something!"

"My dear – of course – how lovely for you!"

"How wonderful! You must be delighted."

"Joyce! My dear!"

The routine was twenty years stale, but they remembered it. They had done it for Mary at eighteen-month intervals over some years, for Florence twice, for Helen once and once for Rose, and countless times for Addie's false alarms before she finally achieved a single son.

"Well," Addie exclaimed, "so we're still at it! Isn't Nature wonderful!"

"Maurice and I are very pleased," Joyce said sedately.

She said this, they knew, expressly on Maurice's behalf. They were unable to comment further. The news needed to be taken home, considered, telephoned about, slept on, before they could present a united front. So they simply enlarged on their congratulations and rose, gathering their belongings.

"Good-bye, then."

"Lovely – lovely."

They pecked each others' cheeks, feeling now that the point of parting was reached, a pang of real regret.

"And take care of yourself, Joyce."

Joyce smiled and said, "That's Maurice's job."

They closed their minds to Rose, dead with her dead child beside her – Maurice's job.

"Maurice is collecting me," Joyce said, "I'll tell him how pleased you all were."

"Yes, dear, do. Tell him we're delighted!"

"And remember, Joyce, there's nothing to worry about. It's the most natural thing in the world." Mary was the authority on child-bearing. "If you want to talk to me about anything, anytime —"

"It's sweet of you, Mary, but I'm not worrying."

They watched Joyce threading her way between the tables as she left them, already setting her feet down the way they remembered they had set their own, proudly, deliberately, a little splayed. She was starting that a bit early, wasn't she?

"It's all very well to say she isn't worrying," Mary said, feeling slighted. "She must remember her own sister."

"She was only ten when Rose died."

Addie said, "Anyhow they don't worry nowadays. It's all explained, full rehearsals, they do it by numbers."

"I could be such a help to her," Mary mourned, "telling her what she ought to get – oh, ever so many ways I could help."

"Those lists! Do you remember?"

"None of that now either. They hand you out a container from the Clinic with everything in it except the baby. A 'Stork Readykit' or something."

"Addie!"

"Perfectly true. There was a young man with one in the bus the other day, labelled for all to see. Such a pale young man, I nearly got up to give him my seat!"

"Addie!"

A little shaken, slight, dissolved, each lady putting as she came down the stairs. and looked at the scented wi them back where they came fro

ADDIE had not come to the tea-party on her bicycle and so she was glad to accept Sarah's offer of a lift home. It was a welcome chance to elaborate on Joyce's news.

"It could be a false pregnancy, of course. Did you think of that? Perfectly possible and much commoner than you'd suppose. Think of Joanna Southcott. Even animals sometimes. There was a spaniel bitch in the Canteen, she had five imaginary puppies – Lord, how she carried on over it, poor dear – and she used to lift them one by one, never made a mistake about the number, and carry them to the same chair at the window every morning. Heaven help anyone who sat down on them. I mean, it could be Joyce's way of getting even with Rose – she must know she's always played second fiddle. Is it a little Shiloh, do you think?"

Waiting for the lights to change Sarah eased the edge of her elastic stocking which was cutting a vicious line in her thigh.

"I don't see why it shouldn't be a fact. Joyce isn't a fool. And she's only forty-one."

"It's inartistic, all the same. We've outgrown labour wards and christenings and matinée coats. Don't think I'm heartless, dear, but I just don't seem to be able to whip up any enthusiasm."

"According to Joyce Maurice is delighted."

"He always has the most reliable reactions. But don't you think it seems out of character for him to be – fruitful?"

It was the right word, and she appreciated Addie's choice of it. Maurice, who was Sarah's cousin, had been the constant piece of male furniture on her girlhood's landscape, included in their schemes or left out of them as it suited. "We can always get Maurice if we have to – you tell him, Sarah." Or "Maurice won't mind staying at home." And after Helen had married the splendid English foreigner, Hubert, Maurice had their approval in marrying Rose – and Joyce, after Rose's death.

"I don't know why we go to these tea-parties," Addie complained briskly, justifying her attendance by her criticism of it. "All over the country there are women like us, Sarah, taking tea with the friends they were at school with. As if that was the only time we'd ever really lived. And thanks to the advances in scientific knowledge we now have false teeth and dyed hair – my dear, Florence! How can she? – and hormone creams and elastic stockings and discreet allowances of phenobarbitone if things get too much for us, so that we can be presentable and not too much bother to anybody while we put in the time till we're old."

"Addie," Sarah scolded, "for goodness sake —"

"I like being melancholy," Addie said. "You have so much zest, you're different. Middle-age is odd. We're not a problem like the young or the very old. No one is exercised about our physical comfort or our morals. And we go out to tea with each other and remember – or invent what we forget. How much do you really remember – Rose, for instance?"

"Of course I remember Rose."

"It was rather suitable, Rose dying. I should have hated her to grow old. But it's a collective thing, we only really remember her when we're together. I wonder if Maurice does. Of course they were terribly in love. Sometimes I get terrified. I race to my desk and pull out the old photographs and stare at all those schoolgirl faces. And now we'll have Maurice's unborn listening in. When is it? Around September, I suppose. Rose was September, too."

They shared the thought of Joyce taking her place at the table, growing monthly more rotund, more podlike with Maurice's child, of the suspense, the emotional involvement they must suffer.

37

"I suppose it's something to look forward to," Addie said, "but it won't be a child of passion, as the saying is. Just the result of habit and accident, don't you think?"

Sarah didn't answer, reluctant and unqualified to speculate on Maurice's private ecstasies.

"How old is Maurice, anyway?"

"He'll be fifty-six."

"A man that age must feel a bit of a fool, specially when they've been married so long. Don't you think, Sarah, that *life* should mean more than that?"

Every ornament on Addie's person vibrated with this enormous little truth. "I mean – *Life*," she repeated.

Long ago Sarah was learning to float. Seawater was beautiful because in it all movements became fluid and graceful, and her body didn't embarrass her but was just a shimmer of flesh clothed in blue-green movement. "I'm floating. Look, Papa, I'm floating!" Papa stood waist-high beside her. The scoop of his striped bathing costume (knee-length, with sleeves to the elbow) revealed his chest, metallic with hair, unfamiliar and exciting. Mama, seated on the rocks buttressed with cushions and rugs, encouraged her. It was one of her better days. "The child's floating, Lilian!" "Splendid, splendid, dear!" thinly from her mother. Miss Fennimore at the water's edge dropped her bunched skirts over white feet and applauded by clapping her hands. A wave took its chance and ran up her legs and she screamed prettily. "Careful," Papa said, male and magnificent. Over Sarah's upturned face a dandelion seed swung on its parachute. Where had it come from? "Look, Papa, a dandelion seed." The wind carried the seed towards the water's surface, caught it again freakishly and lifted it higher, steering it towards the shore. "Will it grow?" The wind had lost interest now, the seed would touch water, would drown. "Will it grow?" She strained her eyes to follow it, hoping it would succeed in the unlikely chance of reaching warm soil, putting down roots, raising leaves.

"I never thought there was much between Maurice and Joyce, did you, Sarah?"

"They're very fond of each other," Sarah said. They had reached Thronehill gate, and she was glad to turn in, to bid Addie good night. Addie went off fussily, wondering aloud how Gerald had been in her absence, if she had been right to leave him, manufacturing a whole range of debates and problems out of what little she had to hand.

Sarah put the car in the garage and walked round to the front of the house. Under her tired feet the small Lough-washed gravel yielded gently. "We will have no graveyard chippings here," Papa declared, "not while we're on top." The gravel had been swept every week by Mr. Boyd, the gardener, and his long brush caressed it into a pattern, as if feathers had stroked the ground. No pattern now, no Mr. Boyd, just tyre-furrows and weeds.

The house stood high above the main road, looking out over lawns and trees to the light-sprinkled waters of the Lough, and to the Castlereagh hills on the further shore. The road might not have been there, except for a murmur of traffic, sufficiently distant to emphasise the isolation. Sometimes a headlight's beam silhouetted the overgrown shrubberies and lent a foreign quality to laurel or rhododendron. Behind the house the shoulder of the Cave Hill was lifted sharply. Clouds pursued each other dizzily over the cliff's face.

Justin's car was at the side of the house and lights shone between the drawn curtains of the stable flat. A light blinked on in Addie's bedroom. Sarah was glad there were no lights waiting for her. She enjoyed solitude and was sorry for those whose lives were lived in a pattern with other people.

She had been undecided about splitting the house up after Papa died. She had a good salary and, thanks to her mother, substantial private means. "You can't live here all by yourself," Maurice said. Reluctantly she agreed, and was glad to discover that the different centres of life the house now

39

contained – Felicity and Justin, Addie and Gerald, and, to her deep joy, Helen – helped to enclose and protect her privacy instead of encroaching on it.

Along the gravel's edge the urns that in bygone summers were always full of geraniums glimmered whitely, and the rustic summer-house yawned on the other side of the lawn. The summer-house had been one of Papa's most notable follies. "A bower! We must have a bower." He wore white flannels and a blazer and sawed and drove nails with much energy and no skill. Mr. Boyd paused over his spade to scratch himself and spit, the silent, scornful professional. "We will call it The Shack!" Papa pronounced when his enthusiasm wore out half-way through. He was always clever at being the first to laugh. The Shack was popular with spiders. With more than spiders.

"Where is your father, dear?"

"I don't know, Mama."

"He said he would read to me."

"You said your head was bad."

"It has cleared now. I think I ought to ask him to read, it was so kind of him. See if you can find him."

She found him in the summer-house against whose uneven roof summer lightning flickered. Miss Fennimore's white dress led the way. As Sarah called it emerged from the dark shape of her father. This was the first time Sarah knew about it. It seemed then the logical consequence of Papa's splendour and Miss Fennimore's eagerness to please.

"Mama says will you come and read, her head is better."

Papa turned slowly, didn't see her for a moment. "Yes, dear, of course."

Tonight a pearly moon rode behind the trees and would soon be clear of them. The animals in the Zoological Gardens were lively. Sarah loved their strange language because it was uncomplicated by any overtones of human relationships or ambiguities of language. Frustration, ferocity, sadness, joy, all reduced to first principles in grunts, yelps, howls, roars. "I like animals better than people," she had confided to Maurice as they lay stretched together along the top of the big chestnut tree, a thousand miles from Mama's drawing-room windows. "You'll fall off," Maurice said. His legs were shorter than hers, though he was older. He had climbed up behind her, doggedly and panting hard, until he was as high as she was. She knew he was frightened and enjoyed knowing it. "Perhaps the tigers have broken loose," she suggested, "and are walking round the bottom of the trees." "Perhaps." But she noticed he did not look down.

Papa and Mama were both in the hall as she let herself in. They crowded round, pressing against her, but she pushed past them. "I'm tired, can't you see? I don't want you. Go away!" She heard them muttering a little as they went.

Surprisingly the door of Helen's flat was lying open.

"Sarah. Sarah – come in, won't you?"

Sarah halted reluctantly. She didn't want to be involved with anyone just now, not even with Helen, and she resented Helen's easy assumption that she would. How did they endure it, people like Mary and Addie and Enid – even Maurice – whose lives were a footpath for other peoples' convenience? It was terrifying. Yet she had been glad and amazed when Helen had taken the flat in Thronehill after Hubert left her. Helen ran a successful flower shop, had smart unusual friends. George was currently her most frequent caller.

"Come in," Helen said, "don't just stand there. Sarah, you ought to buy yourself a new coat, that one is frightful. Now tell me things. What news is there? How were the weird sisters?"

"Weird," Sarah said, and Helen laughed.

She had risen and dressed in a silky negligée and was sitting at a small bright fire. It was a comfortable feminine room, flowers, of course, thick curtains, shaded lights – the kind of room that Sarah would have considered an affectation to provide for herself, even if she had had the taste to furnish it.

41

She was impatient with women who identified themselves with the choice of carpets and cushions and found an emotional, almost an ethical pleasure in the right placing of a picture or a mirror, though Helen, of course, was excused. She noticed that Helen's bed had been smoothed. Helen's face was smooth too, a washed look, the act of grief was over.

"Stay," Helen invited, "have supper with me. Come on – I need company. There's a casserole in the oven. What have you got?"

Sarah admitted to the probability of an egg, trying not to criticise Helen for the casserole she had prepared before she prostrated herself. She agreed to come in, took off her coat and tam, re-skewered her hair.

Helen poured sherry, they sat together at the fire, sipping.

"Thank God I've kept my legs," Helen said, stretching her feet to the warmth. "Better than Florence, anyway. Did you notice Florence's legs – just tubes. Sarah, you never notice anything. Now tell me all the news."

"Joyce is in the family way," Sarah said. She chose the common phrase deliberately, wishing to forestall any amusement from Helen. One of the penalties of loving someone was the anxiety that the person should not make an error in taste, and the careful lengths one must go to, to avoid it.

"Well, well," Helen stroked the silk of her dressing-gown across her knee. "Fancy that! Nothing else?"

Sudden cold anger prompted Sarah to say, "I should have thought it was fairly important when a child is born."

There was a moment's silence before Helen rose abruptly and set down her glass. "Or when one is killed," she said and gripping the edge of the mantelpiece burst into harsh, noisy weeping.

That's it, then. But she will be all right now. Slowly Helen became calmer.

"That's the first thing I've been able to feel all day." She wiped her eyes and tucked her handkerchief away like someone who tidies up after a meal. "That's what happens,

Sarah. You try to keep it alive but you can't. You wait and it doesn't come. It isn't that you forget – I remember every little thing about it – it's just that you don't feel any more."

"I think I know." Sarah had been more touched by this than by Helen's histrionics. "There aren't any more primary colours."

"Something like that. And I'm afraid of being suddenly torn apart, like I was when it happened – and then I blame myself because I'm not."

"Do you suppose Hubert feels like that?"

"Hubert?" Helen shrugged. She never talked about Hubert, and Sarah rarely mentioned him, for she found the relationship between herself and her friends' husbands an uneasy one, as if the girls she knew had grown limbs that they didn't need, and had become less themselves in the process, diminishing by increase. She resented these changes and the willingness with which they made them. Hubert she resented least of all, Glorious Apollo, sufficiently glorious even for Helen. She had been outraged when he walked out on her three years after the little girl was killed.

"I still can't understand why it didn't bring you closer."

How could you explain to Sarah, Helen thought. Tiresome, curious, constant, predictable, clever Sarah, a fossilised schoolgirl, her body still the private unknown thing that it had been when it wore a gym tunic. Go on, tell her about the gentle soft giant who was ready with tenderness when your whole body burned like a torch and tenderness wasn't enough, and who cried quietly at his failures in bed and was so pleased with his small successes. You couldn't explain to Sarah that the act of love became unbearable when it was only a physical exercise that might result in replacing what had been lost, nor would she understand the paralysing shyness this knowledge brought, which made it impossible to go to bed any more.

Sarah was looking at her with the kind clever look that meant she didn't understand. Thank God for Sarah.

43

"Come on, we'll eat."

They shared the meal quietly, enjoying it and each others' company. While they were stacking plates Helen turned on the television and a football match flickered up. A goal was scored, the enormous men ran at each other, leaping, and hugged and kissed.

"Football has become very emotional, don't you think," Sarah said. "I remember once you kissed Rose when she came in first in a relay race, and Miss Hodgkiss said 'Girls, girls!' as if you had done something very dark and terrible."

They laughed gently. Helen switched the set off, brought her knitting, made up the fire. Her hands moved rapidly over the needles, and she fondled the work as she turned each row.

"George was here," Helen said.

"I know, I saw him." All right, she knew she was wearing the face she always did when Helen spoke of George, and of course Helen had seen it and was smiling.

"He left a message that Kitty wanted to see you, and asked if you'd look in tomorrow."

"Was she worse?"

"He didn't say so. I gathered she'd been creating a bit, but I don't think it's urgent."

"I'll call in on my way home from school."

"I think she's inclined to make use of you, don't you, Sarah?"

There was a tone in Helen's voice which Sarah identified joyfully as jealousy, but she remembered Kitty as she had seen her last, her fingers twisting the pink ribbons of her bed-jacket incessantly while her distracted mind fought all the devils in hell at once.

"You shouldn't let her make use of you, Sarah."

"Don't we all make use of each other?"

The sliding wool tightened and the needles stopped. Helen didn't answer. Sarah rose and went to the window, parting the curtains. Justin was leaving, he stood with Felicity

44

in the open doorway of the stable flat. Light poured out, stretching their shadows across the gravel.

"There's Justin, going off. She seems to be by herself a lot, that girl."

"It's no use trying to explain to you," Helen said, "you never felt the way we did."

What way did Sarah feel? Her sufficiency was unreasonable, sometimes irritating. Where did Sarah look for happiness? In the authority she had at school? Yes, probably she got a kick out of that. Entering a class-room in the morning. Thirty girls rise. "Good morning Miss Vincent." Their eyes attentive. What kind of a mood is she in? What will she say today that is funny, outrageous, sarcastic, or unexpectedly and warmly human? What will she do today that will become a school legend? She was a good teacher, and of course there were always girls who would be attracted to her type. And getting those poems of hers published now and again, that must be a help. And there were the conventional sources of delight, stars and sunlight, music, light on water. All the things that were reminders of past ecstasies for Helen were still lively sources for Sarah.

"You never felt the way we did," Helen accused.

Sarah was watching the boy. He put his hands on Felicity's shoulders and waited while she lifted her face.

"Well, did you?"

Their kiss was very gentle and precise, lips closed and laid together, blessing each other, passion recollected in tenderness. They could afford to kiss this way because there would be other times and ways and this discipline was itself a pleasure. Sarah recognised this by sharing the experience in her mind, not through her body which her mind had disqualified as an imperfect instrument. It had always been like this, and had never cost her very much.

At school her evident plainness didn't matter, though she knew about it. But while she earned stars for Latin prose and as long as her English essays were read aloud in class it was

45

enough. The beast grew fat – she had not yet learned to keep him on a chain – and earned for her the reputation of being conceited. Papa and Mama, she knew, expected a different kind of success from her as she grew higher in her teens, but since she knew she was unequipped to achieve it she felt no sense of failure.

And Maurice of course was on her side, and at it, most of the time. His father had been killed on the Somme, his mother had remarried, and now he spent his holidays from school at the house of his uncle and aunt. They were spies together, Maurice and Sarah, into the calf loves of the others. It was a kind of sickness from which they congratulated themselves on being immune. He went to early dances as her partner, they found plenty of scope for research and amusement.

"Have you had a pleasant evening, dear?" Mama's door at the head of the stairs was left open when she was expected home late.

"Oh, yes, Mama."

"Did you dance much?"

"Oh, yes, quite a lot."

"With Maurice?"

"Sometimes with Maurice."

The shaded light at the bedside threw shadows on her mother's hands and wrists and on the humps and hollows where her body was. There was always a little pause now before Mama said, "And who else did you dance with, dear?" Sarah, because she was clever, knew why there was a pause. Her cleverness gave her power over Mama. It was this cleverness that made it possible to reject any image of her mother except the image a child would see, so that it had rarely been necessary to understand or accept her as a whole person.

"Who else, Sarah?"

"I told you – mostly Maurice."

She took the five steps over the carpet, reached the bed and lowered her brow to her mother's pillow to receive the good-

46

night seal, then went into her own room and stared in her mirror at the reflection of her wise eyes in her plain face.

Justin and Felicity had separated and were walking towards the car linked now only by his fingers round her wrist. Sarah knew how the skin of her inner wrist responded to his sliding touch.

"Did you ever feel that way, Sarah?"

"No."

She heard Helen breathe a long breath as if she had got what she wanted. She liked to talk about men and how necessary she found them especially when she wanted to establish a little distance between herself and Sarah. Let her, if it pleases her. Justin's car moved boisterously down the drive. His horn sounded a fanfare as he turned out on to the main road.

"I wonder about those two, don't you?" Helen asked. "She's a sweet girl, I like her. Unexpected of Florence to have a girl like that. She came in the other day – to borrow milk or something – and she saw the wedding group. I don't know why I keep it out, a kind of penance or something, I hate it really. Anyway she asked if she could look at it and who everybody was, and then she said, 'It all seems so very dewy, doesn't it?'"

"Thinking of her own wedding, I suppose. Well, probably a Register Office was more honest."

"It was Florence I was sorry for."

They had all been sorry for Florence when they rallied in full force at the Register Office for her daughter's wedding, trying in that bleak morning air to conjure up a little froth of festivity, some of the peculiar mixture of sentiment and holiness with which their own weddings had been flavoured, and failing badly, conscious only of embarrassment and pity for this scared young man and the heavily pregnant girl who stood on the piece of carpet in front of the office desk and were conducted through the business of marriage but did not look at each other. Only once their hands groped for each

47

other, their fingers tangling. Everyone watching was grateful at least for that.

"All through that ghastly wedding," Helen said, "I was thinking about Oliver. It was like a terrible physical pain, you wouldn't understand. And I suppose it was a waste, and unnecessary."

She wants me to say that it wasn't unnecessary. She envies lovers who go to bed now because they love each other. But she would like to be told that the old arguments are still valid and that love is still a sin that must be blessed in Church.

Papa always sat next the aisle in Church, Sarah next to him, then Miss Fennimore. Mama was too ill to come now. One edge of Sarah's Sunday coat lay against her father's striped trouser, the other brushed the skirt of Miss Fennimore's costume. And God sat on his Throne, Almighty to Save. There was a syllabus set for salvation and rules prescribed.

Since she had seen them together in the summer-house Church services filled her with a mixture of exultation and terror. 'The King of Love my Shepherd is', from her father's easy tenor, and Miss Fennimore's soprano answering, 'I nothing lack if I am His, and He is mine for ever.' Sarah was celebrant of the emotion that linked them. During the sermon she knew how their hands – Papa's on his knees, Miss Fennimore's clasping her hymnbook – enjoyed the knowledge of private communication, the luxury of knowing that each were seen by the other.

The last Sunday was the third in July. The Church was very warm. Many families were on holiday, the three of them sat close together among empty pews. The stained-glass windows blazed and love blazed on each side of her. It was as if two forces of holiness opposed each other. Her father's hands were clenched so tightly that his knuckles were white. Miss Fennimore had taken off her gloves. Her small hands lay palms upward, moving a little, then growing quiet, the fingers open and slack. It can't go on like this. The flowers on the communion table were limp with the heat.

48

It was still hotter in the afternoon. Mama lay in the warm embrace of eau-de-Cologne. Sarah read to her, pausing between sentences for any sign of movement from the silent sun-soaked house.

"Thank you, dear. I think I'll ask Miss Fennimore to come now."

The cow-bell tinkled.

"She can't have heard."

Again the bell.

"She hasn't heard, Mama."

"Perhaps you'd fetch her, dear."

One wondered afterwards if there was not something in Mama's voice. Perhaps she had known.

The morning-room, the drawing-room, the garden, the greenhouse, all empty. Sick with heat and nervousness she knocked at last on Miss Fennimore's door and went in. Sunlight and shadow from the drawn Venetian blinds fell like bars across their bodies, making a cage for their violence.

It was after this that Sarah had what had been known in the family circle as her 'breakdown'. These clever girls – she had been studying too concentratedly for her Matric. She had spent a long period of unmoving weeks at the house of an aunt who lived at a seaside resort on the south coast of England. She wasn't either happy or unhappy, exempt from emotion or judgement – even from relationships – first out of shock and apathy, and then by a deliberate act of withdrawal which she cultivated once she had learned it. She took daily walks along the promenade, oblivious of the crowds of holiday makers. She didn't notice their absence in the autumn when they went back to the city and the promenade and strand were empty. She was already established in isolation.

She was summoned home at the end of November. Nurses had replaced Miss Fennimore. Her mother died the following summer. There was no mention of Miss Fennimore, no trace, no sign. Papa's loving care for her mother seemed to indicate that he had done a calculation in ethical mathematics and had cancelled Miss Fennimore out. Years later, after Papa's death, Sarah had a letter from her. She recognised the writing, remembering it from labels on Christmas presents and at birthdays. '*With dearest love to Sarah, from Gwen Fennimore.*' They had always been gay and unpredictable presents. The writing had altered very little. '*I have learned with real grief of the passing of your dear Papa . . . memories of those happy years which I passed in your house . . . such kindness.*' Now Miss Fennimore lived at the seaside in a Home for elderly ladies. The air was good. Sarah visited her every year.

"I'll tell you something," Helen said. "No – don't go away. I want to tell you. Oliver and I were going away together on his next leave. We'd arranged it, it was all arranged. We couldn't go on the way we were, it was like burning alive. It didn't matter who I hurt. And when I heard he was dead there was part of me that said, 'I'm glad. Now I can't do it.' As if I'd been let off something – excused – do you understand? That's the thing I remember most."

Helen was at the dressing-table, talking over her shoulder. Sarah hadn't turned from the window. I wish she would stop. What does she expect me to say? She likes to do this to me. Does she know I am filled with panic and a sort of disgust at the idea of a middle-aged woman wondering why she hadn't gone to bed with a man she loved twenty years ago? There were hundreds like them. His body had burned out, in the sky over Germany, it would be more decent if her own had done the same. In any case it was Hubert she loved. I know. I was at the wedding. There could be no more beautiful and intimate truth than the truth in their faces as they took the vows in Church.

Helen was doing something to her face, pouting her mouth, consoling her reflection in the mirror lovingly.

"I've got to go," Sarah said, her mind twisting a little. "A stack of exercises for tomorrow —"

"Must you?"

"I must."

Whatever response Helen had conjured from the mirror had done her good. "Poor Helen," she smiled, "left all alone."

This was a drill Sarah knew. Helen was a child who hopes to be comforted by being bullied. It gave her her exit line.

"You behave yourself," she said, "and no more crying. Promise?"

"I promise," Helen said, and Sarah left her.

CHAPTER FOUR

MAURICE walked up Sarah's drive briskly with the books that were his excuse for the errand tucked under his arm. He had not yet fully justified his visit to himself. There was no light from the window of her study – how tiresome it would be if after all his inward debate she wasn't there! Maurice liked life to fall in with the plans he had for it and thought it should, since they were rarely extravagant or demanding. He had decided to walk rather than take the car, to give himself time to clarify his approach.

"I want to pop round to Sarah's with some books," he told Joyce who was sitting with her feet up – wasn't that a little Victorian? He had a feeling that Joyce was overplaying the whole thing. Even Truby King – no, he closed that door of thought firmly. Rose had subscribed fully to the gospel according to Truby King.

"I would have taken them this afternoon if you'd told me," Joyce said, opening her eyes widely the way she often did, "but perhaps they'd have been too heavy."

She was overplaying it. He didn't know whether to criticise or encourage her. The prospect of parenthood had taken him utterly by surprise. He thought the act of begetting ought to be a deliberate one, at least one should be able to be currently informed. He was also a little anxious in case anyone was going to be amused. Of course his students would be, but he expected that, and already the prospect pleased him faintly. there was one pert blonde in the front row whose reaction would be delicious. Some of his students were parents already. But his contemporaries? Surely the loss of first wife and child twenty-five years ago would warn them? Not that this was in any sense a repetition of anything that had happened before. When the coffin closed on Rose with the crumpled anonymous baby on her breast it completed an experience that was unique. Sometimes when he looked at Joyce now– that mild version of his dear love, sufficiently mild never to tempt comparison – he felt a sense of elation for the child she was carrying – and then became stiff with fright, grudging her her prim and joyful pregnancy, and unwilling to beome involved in it.

"They'd have been much too heavy for you," he said and bent to lay his mouth against her forehead, killing emotion with this routine act of tenderness. She smiled and reached for his hand and held it close against her cheek.

"Dear Maurice. I love you. I love you when you look at me that way."

"What way?"

"Brooding – like a cellist. You should have played the cello, you have the face."

"Do you think I've missed my vocation?"

He took his hand from hers and turned to examine his face in the mirror on the wall behind her; he knew what she meant. It was an academic face that suited his profession, but squarer than the traditional face of a scholar. Even in sailor suits Maurice had been distinguishably Napoleonic. When he was a student he had even cultivated for a time the lock of hair. Now the hair on his temples had receded and the lock was a lone tuft. Brooding, Joyce called his face. He watched himself smile, savouring the success of this and ignoring the rest of himself, his plump shabbiness, his boyish middle-age, the arms and legs that had always been a little too short.

"It could look like you," Joyce said. She had swivelled round and was watching him. "I hope it does."

"Do you?"

He tried to hide his irritation. The thought had risen just as she spoke, he would have liked to consider it privately. Joyce had changed since she knew about the baby. Sharper, more perceptive, making more claims on him. He didn't think he cared for the change.

"Maurice, I wish you'd seen their faces when I gave them the news." She laughed prettily, twisting her fingers through her beads. "I kept it right to the end – was that very naughty of me? Anyhow, they were wildly surprised."

"Were they? I shouldn't have thought it was so very improbable." He criticised his voice because it sounded pompous and faintly offended.

"You are funny, darling."

"Am I?"

He wanted very much to ask for fuller details about how the news had been received, what they had said, who had said it. But he didn't want her to think that it mattered, since they often made fun together of these reunion tea-parties. And so he went off to Sarah's house, to find out for himself.

The study light flicked on as he entered the porch and rang the bell. So she was in. By this time his eagerness had got out of hand and he was glad it was dark. It was easier in the dark to reclaim the welcome and sense of permanence which Thronehill had always held for him. A place of refuge from boarding school which he hated, being something of a pretty boy in spite of the Napoleonic exterior. Here on holiday he had been happy in the company of peculiar, aggravating Sarah, and in the ordered life of the household, old-fashioned, provincial, detached a little from the shocks and changes even of its generation.

As he entered the porch he smelt the eloquent scent of geraniums, though he knew these were not there any more. The inner door was heavy, with an upper panel of opaque glass, on which a design of Ceres bearing her cornucopia was engraved. He knew the contents of it, down to each head of wheat, each bunch of grapes. He had a passion for enumerating things when he was a boy; things were counted again and again. Ceres was a handsome suburban matron in decent draperies, serene, severe. He had always identified her with his aunt, Sarah's mother, whom he loved for lack of his own. He didn't like Sarah's father, whose exuberance offended him.

The light in the hall was lit, and Ceres shone out to welcome him before she was obscured by Sarah's familiar bulk.

She peered out short-sightedly. "Who is it?"

"The Marquis of Carrabas!" he announced with a flourish, giving her childhood's cue which might be most useful to him since sincerity was dangerous.

He was disappointed. "Oh, it's you, Maurice," she said grumpily, "well, you'd better come in, I suppose."

She headed up the stairs, he followed. God, those legs, those hips, how do women bear it? Not that Sarah would care. The texture of the banister rail under his hand, the stairs' gentle ascent and the breadth of the half-landing gave him some of the welcome that he hadn't got from her.

"I'm always glad you didn't change the house any more than you had to, Sarah," he said.

She rounded the turn. "It's falling to pieces." Her deep voice sounded like a dirge. "To pieces, to pieces."

Her study was untidy like it always was, and cold. She had neglected to draw the curtains across the window and the pane of glass bleakly reflected back the electric light. There were no flowers. A pile of exercise books sprawled over the table. He thought of Joyce, relaxed and soft on the frilled chesterfield in front of a well-tended fire. Surely Sarah could do more about it? He sat angrily on the chair she indicated and nursed his books.

She set her own chair squarely opposite his. He had interrupted her and so she intended to conduct the interview along her own lines.

"Well, Maurice? What have you come for?" And while her eyes examined him he studied her plain strong face and flat hair, and long nose, the too-emphatic mouth in the narrow chin, and took some satisfaction from identifying a few hairs that lay undeniably on her upper lip.

55

"Joyce says she told you the news," he said, feeling vexed with her and with himself.

Of course he shouldn't have come. It was a bad error in judgement. But the habit of sharing news with Sarah persisted. He wanted her reaction, hoped for her blessing. Maurice had learned to bolster himself against life's assaults, and had persuaded himself that the immunity he achieved was in fact evidence of maturity. It was a relief to be excused from shocks and fears and ecstasies. But now? Justify me, Sarah, justify my jubilation. Make it all right for me.

"You were surprised, Joyce says."

"Indeed we were." Pause.

"I think Joyce is very pleased," he hazarded.

He was quite unprepared for the sudden movement with which she leaned forward and laid her large cold hand on his for a moment. He felt moved, remembering how rarely she touched anyone and how much she criticised demonstrativeness in others – 'all that stroking and petting and talking into other peoples' faces'.

"You must both be pleased. I think it's wonderful news, Maurice."

His heart kindled. "You do?" Go on, Sarah, go on, say something else.

"I will be a little old for a father, don't you think?"

He prayed for her to contradict him. Or let her mock him a little and he would be ready to join in and mock himself.

"Some fathers are much too young."

"I shall be old enough to be his grandfather."

"His?"

"It could be a son."

"Is that what you want?"

"I think so."

"Well, then, I hope it will be a son."

He leaned forward, drawing his chair nearer so that his knees were almost touching her.

"I can't tell you how I feel, Sarah."

56

He wanted very much to be able to tell her. He wanted words. He wanted to say impossible, irrevocable things. 'Share this with me. Celebrate my son. Put out flags for me, Sarah. I have created a child in a woman's body. I have created life. I want to feel awe and wonder, and delight – the way we felt these things together when we were children. If I am unable to feel these things I will be frightened. Give me back the glory.'

If he hadn't known her so well he would have missed the tightening of her nostrils, that look on her face, distaste, retreat. He sat upright and moved away.

"You don't understand."

"I do. Of course I do."

It was no use. The old maid's look. It pleased him to label it. *Virgo Intacta*. He'd been a fool to come. There wasn't anything he needed from her.

"It's wonderful, Maurice. I'm so very pleased, for you and for Joyce."

How much had she forfeited to preserve this frightening completeness, this God Almighty act, so graciously pleased because his wife was to have a child? What had she paid for this cleverness of hers that made her immune and permitted her to make judgements? That time she was away so long, before her mother's death – they said she was ill – something had happened to Sarah then. She had come back changed, withdrawn, critically amused. Not needing other people.

After a few mechanical exchanges he rose to go. At least he had not been tempted to become emotionally obstetric. He was grateful to make his getaway without that.

He reclaimed his solemn hat, pecked her cheek – how odd to kiss a woman and not be conscious of perfume – and bade her good night.

"Don't come down," he said flatly, as they stood together at the head of the staircase. "There isn't any need. I'll let myself out."

57

Moonlight streamed in through the open landing window. Up in the Zoo a lion roared.

"Be careful as you go past the rhododendrons," she warned, taking refuge in a joke because the interview had flopped and she wanted to redeem it a little. "Listen to the lions – this is their night out."

"I'll be careful," he promised without humour.

He had reached the hall and was crossing it when Addie trotted out from her flat.

"Maurice! Maurice my dear! Well, this is nice!"

She advanced, gripping his arms and pushing her face into his.

"Maurice, were you actually going off without giving me the chance to congratulate you? You were, you know! You needn't say you weren't! Well I call that plain mean. This is wonderful news, I can't tell you how I felt! It isn't just you and Joyce, my dear, if you know what I mean – this is news for all of us. And Gerald's thrilled, just thrilled. I'd ask you in so that he could tell you so himself, but this isn't one of his good days. But he was simply thrilled!"

Silly woman. Silly babbling woman. But in spite of this her kindness warmed him, and he felt himself respond.

"Thank you, Addie. Thank you very much."

"There aren't any words," Addie crooned, "there just aren't any words!"

"I know. Joyce and I feel like that." He smiled at her, praying that she might be rewarded and Sarah punished.

"Sarah would be able to find words."

Addie lifted her head and he knew without looking up that Sarah was still standing on the upper landing, observing them. Damn Sarah. That was what she used to do when at last he succeeded in shedding her at dances to look for other partners and find Rose. She had stared, squatting partnerless on the stairs, ugly, calm, self-sufficient. Other girls who were without partners put up a busy show of chatter among themselves. Sarah only glowered and gazed, contentedly single. He had

58

been grateful when her father's long illness finally released him from her, so that she had not presided over the three years that he had with Rose.

"You'd know what to say to him, Sarah!" Addie cried up the stairs.

"Do you think so?" Sarah's robust contralto sounded amused and indifferent.

"A stake in immortality, that's it, Maurice," Addie breathed, leaning more intimately towards him, "hackneyed, I know – but there are some things you can only say in one way, don't you agree?"

He agreed willingly without giving her a chance to try out any variations, unwound her fingers from his lapel and maintained his smile until he was through the door and out across the shallow step.

The smell of the shrubbery and the dry furtive leaves that had hidden in the autumn and only emerged with March winds to blow round his feet comforted him a little. There were no lions in the rhododendrons. He had reached the gate and was turning into the road before he remembered that the books he had brought for Sarah were still under his arm.

Addie took her time in closing the door after he had gone. This was to give Sarah a chance to go back to her own flat. It was a pity that she hadn't realised earlier that Sarah was up there, overhearing what she said, and she felt herself guilty of extravagance – treachery, perhaps – considering what she had said to Sarah about Joyce and her news. Sarah was so relentlessly critical, so uncompromising. She would never understand how it was possible to be one thing to one person and another quite different thing to someone else and be sincere to both of them. Sarah was always the same with every one – except perhaps with Helen. Those two made you wonder. Sarah so masculine, poor dear, and Helen of course had always been the sexy type. There had been others visiting her flat before George.

But the little extravagant encounter with Maurice had done

59

Addie good, a lot of good. She felt enriched and liberated by it, and she didn't want any comment from Sarah to spoil it for her. What was life, after all, unless you allowed yourself to feel? I mean – Life? Of course Sarah was clever, one admired her very much, but sometimes her cleverness repelled, like those curious verses of hers. Poetry should surely, Addie thought, be a little warmer, more intimate than that? Her own writing was. It was Addie's dream to find a publisher for her essays – 'my little pieces' – and one of her diversions in idleness was to compose obscure dedications for the fly-leaf and to invent romantic explanations for them. 'For C.C.P. – Remembering the Afternoon when it Rained.' 'To R.L. – Who was Right, after All.' Something along those lines.

There was no voice or movement from the landing above, and Addie regained her own flat without interruption and made Gerald his hot drink and took it into the bedroom for him. Then she carried hers to the sitting-room fire, and while she drank it thought warmly of Maurice and this late evidence of his virility.

Then it was time to write her weekly airmail letter to Alistair, her son, that dull product of the most colourful event of her life. She had been in labour with him for thirty-one hours. He had been a quiet orderly baby, had never given her the opportunity to wear herself out over him, to be the epic maternal animal smelling of breast-milk and talc. From a stodgy little boy he had grown into a stodgy young man. His childhood had been a great disappointment to his mother; there were no fairies at the bottom of his garden, not a breath of whimsy, no Mother Fixation, no teenage problems, no delicious wildness. The strongest feeling he displayed was his disapproval of his mother's enthusiasms. Even when she used to take him to the pantomime she knew she clapped too loudly. He was in Canada now, mildly and quietly successful. So she wrote him a restrained catalogue of the week's events, suppressing out of consideration for him all underlinings and exclamation marks, and was glad the Airmail form set limits for her.

She was tired, too, feeling that pain again, remembering the medical book and chasing the idea out of her mind by recalling the paragraph that deplored the number of women who worried when there wasn't any case for worry.

It was time then for the news. This was the announcer she liked best, her special one. Dapper and yet so kind. They smiled at each other. He was wearing that tie again. What a mess Africa was in. And another air crash; you could always tell by his voice – how beautiful in the tragic modulations! – when something like an air crash was coming. He made a little crack about the weather before he said good night. "You're frisky, aren't you?" she said affectionately, as she switched him off.

Half an hour later she knelt at the side of the bed to say her prayers to the God who wore the announcer's face. When she was a little girl He had worn the face of Moses in the stained-glass window in Church. She herself had not been conscious of the transfer. She asked not to be led into temptation, regretting privately that there was so little chance, and to be delivered from evils with which she would willingly have engaged. Then she slid between the sheets, curving herself to the cold curve of Gerald's body. There was never any warmth from Gerald's body.

"Is it bad tonight, dear?"

She slid her hand up the back of his pyjama jacket.

"So so."

Her hand moved consolingly over his thin cold shoulders. "That better?"

He grunted assent.

"Maurice was here."

"Maurice?"

"To see Sarah."

"Not so hard, dear."

She massaged more gently. Her palm passing across his dry

61

skin made a light rasping noise. It reminded her of a shantung dress she had once possessed. Just the same texture and noise. Shantung – and piqué – and then there was spongecloth and something short-lived called ratine; and after that there was cretonne – huge patterns like wall-paper, a bird of paradise on your bosom and a floral urn on your behind – and organdie later on.

"That's the place," Gerald said. "That's right on it."

"Maurice and Joyce – it's thrilling, don't you think? I mean, we're apt to imagine that sort of thing is over. It isn't of course. There was a bit in a magazine I was reading the other day. We shouldn't think it is over, should we? Should we, Gerald?"

"A little to the left, dear."

Her hand changed direction without breaking the rhythm. She thought briefly of Maurice and Joyce, moving together in bed. She tried not to blame Gerald. He had his lapses sometimes. About four times a year he went out without explanation and came home blind drunk. To Addie these episodes had a certain dark attraction, they lent colour to his life and hers. She could see them coming, knew the symptoms, watched the restlessness (like pre-menstrual tension) building up in him to the inevitable climax, felt strong forces of emotion flow from her when she opened the door and found him swaying on the step, helped him to vomit, put him triumphantly to bed, brooded over him, her man, her child.

"I mean, Gerald, you remember how you felt about Hedda when she was here? I mean, it was obvious, did you think I didn't notice? Did you – really? Of course she was gorgeous. I was glad – no, really I was. I didn't blame you a bit. 'A dish', that's what they say nowadays, isn't it? She was 'a dish'. What would we have said, Gerald? 'A nice bit of fluff?' Something terrible like that?"

"More or less, I suppose."

There was no response from him at all.

62

"It sounds terrible, simply terrible – something out of the Ark. Do you get frightened, Gerald, when you think how old we are? Do you?"

"Not much."

"We're not really old, are we?"

"It depends what you call old."

"What do you call old?" Let us have a conversation, let us argue, discuss, debate, speculate, theorise, contradict each other, agree perhaps, or find reasons why we don't agree. He didn't answer.

"Some people go on much longer than others," she said, taking her fingers across his spine a little viciously, "Maurice and Joyce for instance."

"That's enough. That's done it, dear."

He hunched his shoulder, drawing the sheet tight about it, and turned to his side of the bed, burrowing in the pillow. Now he will go through the procedure of falling asleep. She knew every breath of it.

"Good night, Googoo."

"Good night, Booboo," she said rebelliously.

The pain in her own body had faded. Across the sharp ridge of his back she watched the moon travelling over the sky, a complacent shantung-coloured orb. "Is this all there is?" she asked it, "has it all happened? Why can we not lie in each others' arms in the moonlight and talk tantalisingly of death?"

It was unfair still to be hungry when the meal was evidently over. It hadn't been an impressive meal for Addie, though she had done her best to appreciate what was offered to her. All her life she had lain in wait for ecstasies, enthusiasms, dilemmas, disasters, and had invented them for herself when events had not obliged. What huge blossoms of frustration and despair Chekhov could have raised from her boredom! She respected Chekhov, so much better than the sexy plays on television nowadays, with the man's hand travelling up the girl's skirt and neither of them finding a word to say. A little bit of poetic commentary, Addie thought, made passion so much more civilised.

Somewhere in the house a telephone purred four times and was answered. A peculiar time to ring. Curiosity and envy niggled. She heard the telephone ring again just before Gerald reached the point of rolling on to his back, which he always did when he had slept for twenty minutes. The moonlight lent his face importance, as the uniform had done when she had met him first.

On the edge of sleep his hand groped for her, but she turned away, and invented a new, extravagant and delicious dedication for her volume. The telephone rang for the third time just before she slept.

CHAPTER FIVE

WHEN Sarah had left her Helen went straight into her beauty drill. She wanted to be finished before the call came through. It was always late when he rang, so that he could be sure no one was with her. She had no wish to be caught with a make-up turban twisted round her head, greasy-faced and slippery-fingered. Even though he wouldn't know it made a difference to her to feel that she looked right. Otherwise she wouldn't be able to play it properly. You didn't argue with vanity at fifty, you gave in, all the time.

This performance with creams and oils and lotions was a celebration of comfort. Her hands rotated caressingly; how many inches of the stuff had she sunk into her skin? It didn't help her very much, but it left her feeling good, soft, perfumed, a form of love-making. It pleased her to care for what was left of her beauty, as if it were something external to herself, something in trust, to which she owed duty and attention, as she might have done to a child. What was there in a man's world to compensate for this kind of self-indulgence? Pipe-sucking? The passive contemplation of young girls' legs?

When the smoothing, patting, splashing was finished she slid back her dressing-gown so that her bosom and shoulders were bare. The skin was creamy and firm, the orbs of her shoulders shone with the muted sheen of egg-shell. She put her palms below her breasts to raise them, then lifted her chin, and with half-closed lids smiled at her reflection. The success of this was so suddenly painful that she folded her arms across her body, rocking, as if she were holding a child who cried for something he couldn't have. I want. I want. What chance have you got? Look at yourself. She turned the shaded light so that it fell squarely on her face.

It shouldn't happen like this, this fading, creasing, ageing, dulling, thickening, all taking place so slowly that you could cheat yourself, if you were clever, until you realised one day that the old face was a caricature of the young face still recognisable behind it. There should be a day set aside for celebrating beauty and being finished with it. This is the last day I will be beautiful. See how beautiful I am! And after that a blind would come down and a certificate issued – To Whom It May Concern: the bearer of this Certificate was once young and lovely. The air moved gently round her and the wind was never in the east. A chime of bells rang when she went into a room, men reading their newspapers in crowded buses looked up and saw her and sucked the insides of their cheeks, waiters quickened their step for her, and milliners' assistants when she had left the shop tried on the hats that she had tried on and frowned at their reflections.

Her beauty treatment had comforted her and so had Sarah. There was always Sarah. Why not? The appetite for admiration didn't die. You were forced, half-ashamed, to rummage for it wherever you could get it. In any case whatever it was between herself and Sarah it went deeper than she cared to admit. Whoever else you lost Sarah was constant.

And Sarah never interfered with the game she played, or criticised. That was because she knew the game existed but didn't understand it. How she had shied at the mention of Oliver. That was like Sarah. Oh yes, go to bed with a man if you want to, but don't talk about it, not to me. Probably Sarah envisaged passionate love-scenes played out in this room between George and herself. A middle-aged orgy. George knew the game as well as Helen did, and they played it for their mutual consolation. Forgive my thickened face and I will forgive the skin that has tightened on the bridge of your nose and sagged over your throat. Don't ask too much. When we go to bed let passion be tender, and afterwards let us smile and be wise and a little sad. Shock me with verbal intimacies, I like that. Keep the light burning between us.

It wouldn't burn much longer. They had played it carefully but they were nearly through. Helen knew the signs, probably he did, too. A small impatience quickly concealed, a moment's inattention, a contrived quarrel from which they could leap into a reconciliation. Helen would be careful to cast off first. It would be a pity, she was very fond of George, she had enjoyed him. There would of course be someone else; there always was. In a flower shop she was a sitting target. With sudden panic she thought, 'There must be someone else. I don't know how to live without it. I shall end up in an Old Peoples' Home conducting a violent affair with an elderly gentleman whose body warms a little when we sit in the sun together. If Hilary had lived she would have saved me from this final idiocy. She could have had her first child by now.'

The anniversary of Hilary's death was the event in her calendar which she dreaded most and observed most scrupulously, probably because here God had been wholly to blame, unlike the loss of Oliver or Hubert's desertion. It was like taking out an old dress from a wardrobe and trying it on. Look, I haven't grown out of it. She was killed in the street when she fell off her bicycle. She was nine years old. I haven't forgotten. She opened her eyes once in the Hospital. I remember. There is nothing to be gained by doing this, but it seems the most honest thing I can do, an insurance against sorrow staling into sentiment, a positive effort at sincerity.

There was still the telephone, after that she could sleep. She laid two sleeping tablets beside her bed and then a third as a guarantee that she wouldn't need it, and put the little bottle back in the drawer. As she slid it into place the telephone rang.

"Hold the line, please. I have a call for you from London."

She sat on the edge of the bed, pleating the silk of her dressing-gown while she waited, resenting the heightening tension.

At last she heard his voice.

"Helen – are you there, Helen?"

"Hallo, my dear."

The endearment was easy if you slipped it in right away.

"I hope this is a convenient time to call you."

"Yes, of course."

He had not asked if it was a convenient time to walk out on her. He has got a little pompous in his middle-age, she thought, pleased that the thought could amuse her. Splendour sometimes stiffens into pomposity.

"Good to hear your voice, Helen."

"And yours."

The opening sentences were always like this, every time, dicey, groping for direction.

"How have you been, Helen? What news is there?"

"Nothing very unusual."

"The business?"

"Fairly brisk thank you. How are you, Hubert?"

"Just a year older," he said.

There was something different about his voice. He generally said 'a year older' as if he didn't give a damn. This time she wasn't sure.

"Aren't we all?"

"My flowers, they arrived, did they?"

She pressed her knees together to stiffen herself. "Yes. They were there yesterday when I went up with my own."

"What sort of a day was it?"

"Fine. That hard spring sunshine. All purple and gold on the Lough. And the seagulls, of course." Perhaps this was a sentimental embroidery, but one has to say something. There must be something one can find to say.

After a moment he said, "I thought of you."

"Thank you." She was glad that had been said, and it was over.

His voice sounded as if he was glad, too. "Now tell me everything. How's the flat? How's Sarah?"

"Exactly how you left her."

She appreciated his amusement.

"And the flat?"

"I've been doing it up."

"Business must be brisk."

Again his voice was not as she had expected it. A trace of envy? She pushed the idea from her mind quickly before it could take root.

She asked firmly, "And how is Elspeth?"

After a moment he said, "I wondered if perhaps you hadn't heard."

She felt sick in her stomach. "Heard about what? What do you mean?"

"Elspeth left me in August."

"She left you?"

"Yes."

Did she leave you on a shining summer morning? Did the front door bang and did you run to the window quickly for no reason you could explain and see her back receding down the path, her arm straightened with the weight of the suit-case?

"I see," she said trying to keep her voice level and breathe properly. "No, Hubert, I hadn't heard."

"I thought perhaps you might."

"No. I hadn't."

"I wasn't sure."

This is a maze, we go round and round.

"I'm sorry, Hubert," she said.

He didn't answer.

"I am very sorry."

"Christ's sake, who asked you to be sorry? You never knew her."

She longed to tell him how well and how gratefully she knew Elspeth in her imagination, loyal and colourless and very loving, and how much she would have welcomed his assurance that her guess was correct. Elspeth had no right to leave him. She had taken on the job of Hubert and she should have seen it through.

69

Her hand tightened on the receiver to check the trembling, and when she closed her eyes for a moment she had a clear picture of Hubert's hand tightening, that large, gentle, ineffectual hand.

"I'm sorry," he said after a pause. "Helen, I'm damn sorry. I think perhaps I am a little drunk."

There were sounds that could have been weeping. It is my turn now to ask who is keeping the house for him, who looks after his shirts and goes to bed with him, who is his assurance, his mild warmth, who lives the other half of his life for him, the way I used to do. But when she didn't speak he said, "Goodbye Helen," and all at once the line was dead.

She took the three sleeping pills and before she went to bed turned to the mirror and saw her face looking out at her with a kind of frightened inquiry.

Down in the stable flat Felicity lay on the bed, one shoe kicked off, too tired to kick off the other. She pressed her backbone into the mattress trying to ease the aching pain in it. She hadn't wanted to do that crazy Charleston, she was tired enough before that. Justin should have noticed how tired she was. She felt silly, anyhow, and messy, in her old slacks and flatties and the crumpled apron still tied round her.

"Come on! I'll show you!"

"Hush, you'll wake him!"

"Oh, come on!"

He took the bowl of congealing baby-food out of her hand and put it down with a flourish that knocked a pile of nappies off the table.

"Come on!"

For a moment or two she had been caught up in his enthusiasm, forgetting how tired she was, how sluttish, matching her skill to his own, knowing that his eyes applauded her. This is fun. This is the way it used to be. But her fingers felt rough against Justin's smooth ones, and soon her breasts became painful and hot with the movement. They were big already for the evening feed. "You've got it, you've got it!" And then just as he pulled her towards him – he could never remember about her breasts – the baby whimpered and at once all the gaiety went out of his face and he dropped her hands and the dance was over.

"Poor baby, poor little boy, poor baby!" she chanted, standing beside the cot, starting the rhythmic rocking that sometimes appeased him. But the yelling grew more insistent, and she lifted the furious flannelled body and held him close against her, glad that it hurt, knowing that Justin was watching, and that he criticised her for turning so quickly to the baby.

"He never misses a trick, does he?"

"Then come and tell him to behave himself," she challenged, mouthing the down on the baby's moist head. "Come on, Pop, do your stuff!"

"That mother's boy!" he mocked. He said he was going down to the pub and did she mind and of course she said she didn't.

"But I thought you were going to work for your exam."

"Fat lot of a chance to work with that going on."

The baby quietened and she put him back in his cot. She knew by the way Justin kissed her when he went off that he was already ashamed at what had happened and angry with himself because he had to be ashamed. The fanfare of his horn told her that he was glad to be out of the house. She meant to wash her hair, paint her nails, lie long in a perfumed bath, but all she had done was sprawl on the bed staring at the ceiling. Tired, tired, tired. Twice she got up to bend over the baby's face because she couldn't hear him breathing. She put her face low enough to feel the warm quick breath against it. Although he slept his hands still moved fussily, fighting against nothing.

When the telephone rang she heaved herself up and made a grab for it, but stopped, smiling, with fingers outstretched, and waited until it had purred eleven times. Let him wait a moment. Let him be sorry. Then she snatched the receiver fiercely with both hands and said, "Darling."

"Bitch. Why did you let me go on ringing?"

On the phone Justin's voice was light, teasing, playing a game and knowing you would play it back, a lover's voice like it had been a year ago, as if there was a flame between their faces.

"I rang and rang," he said. "Who have you got with you in the flat?"

She giggled and made quick little kisses. "Perhaps I was cleaning my oh-so-beautiful teeth. Or Giving Myself Tomorrow's Loveliness Today!"

"Perhaps you weren't."

"I love you, I love you, I love you, I love you," she recited.

He said, "I love you," gravely, so that her heart turned over. "Anyhow, you ought to be careful what you say when you answer the phone at this time of night. For all you knew it could have been some lechy old man."

"Sweet, you are funny. You've been reading the papers."

"No. Honestly. Ask Sarah – she's been having trouble."

"Sarah? Did she tell you?"

"She asked my expert advice."

"I don't believe you. What did you tell her?"

"I gave her a way of dealing with the trouble, absolutely foolproof, under plain cover, money back if unsatisfied, patent applied for."

"You're crazy. What did you say?"

"Never you mind. Look, there's a good crowd here tonight. Couldn't you come along?"

"You know I couldn't."

"Just for half an hour."

"No, Justin."

"Give me one good reason."

"All right. The baby." Some day one of us will have to start calling him by his name, and make a person out of him.

"Ask old Sarah to come in. She'd come if you asked."

"She doesn't know anything about babies."

"Not like you!"

She was too tired even to feel hurt. Maybe it was just another joke. She was tired all the time now. Heaven, just now, was a bed, a bed to herself and silence – no, heaven was Justin's body hard on her own, the ceiling palely luminous and the baby fast asleep – no, heaven was the baby coming to her breast, warm and little and hungry.

Justin hadn't had the baby, the long months, the fright of a tightening body, skin stretched and shiny and navel distended like a bubble, the pain or the drugging weakness, like a kitten washed up on the beach. He thought the baby was a parcel you could dump with a stranger until you were ready to collect it, not a piece of you torn away.

"Come on," he urged, "there are some luscious blondes here. Come and look after me. Remember your wifely duty."

"I can't."

There was a pause before he said, "I don't know why I bothered to ring."

"I'm sorry."

He said, "Not to worry," so gently and unexpectedly that desire poured all through her painfully.

"Perhaps I could ask Mummy tomorrow."

"Mummy would love it, of course." He made it a baby word, smacking his lips.

Poor Mummy. Mummy would have liked a wedding like the one in the photograph in Helen's flat, the line-up of relations in best clothes with a solemn look on their faces that made them all look a little alike. That sort of a wedding. Dewy – sacrificial. Clouds of white tulle floating behind her and a long long aisle stretching out in front. Justin waiting at the end of it, strange and a little alarming. Music from the organ pouring over them, and the voice of the minister tying them together, for ever, whether they were happy or unhappy, whatever happened to them, so that if love died on them habit took its place and bound them as closely as love

73

had, until years and years ahead when they were very old one of them died and it was over. And after the wedding a Hotel bedroom for the honeymoon with a great white bed like an altar and a dream-nightie and a shaded light, instead of a sofa in a back room during a party with her clothes half on and terrified in case anybody would come.

The baby stirred; he was opening his mouth.

"I've got to hang up now, Justin."

"I suppose he's mewling again."

"Just going to."

"Hope he doesn't puke. Good-bye."

She put the receiver down, dizzy with fatigue, and turned rebelliously to the cot. The baby's calm eyes were open, he had decided against crying. He considered his mother. Poor little creature, she thought, what do I do about you? I am the most important influence in your life, do you know that? I have to teach you how to wipe your nose and do your buttons and say thank you, and later on your letters and your manners and not to love me too much, and your prayers perhaps. Mummy still says her prayers. I've seen her from the landing, kneeling at the side of the bed with her hair clamped in a hair-net, putting items on the agenda for God's urgent consideration. 'Our Father'. Justin's your father, down at the pub with the glamorous blondes.

The baby was asleep again. If she went to bed she could sleep too. Then she would be rested when Justin came; she would wake feeling the thrust of his body and his hands. It would be easier if she could sleep a little first.

Up in her study Sarah still worked her way through the Latin exercises, with enjoyable authority. The window was open, she had not yet drawn the curtain. She could see the swing of shafting light from the headlights as they rounded the curve of the road, the bland face of the moon. The last of the cross-Channel steamers, like a string of lighted beads, had gone down the Lough. There were fewer voices from the Zoo. The green biro commended and criticised. The move-

74

ments in the house, Felicity's baby wailing and quietening, Addie putting out the cat, Helen's bath-water, had all enclosed her more securely in agreeable isolation.

After the exercises a pile of English essays. These were pleasant too. They were from a class she hadn't previously taught and she had set them the old old title 'These I have Loved'. It was a procedure that produced unfailingly useful results. Read the poem first in class, that young man's self-conscious catalogue of personal darlings, then set the essay. Your own list – the Things You Love. And from the essays she would learn more about each girl than she could find out in a couple of terms' class-room acquaintance. 'Miss Vincent takes a pride in knowing each of her pupils individually' her Head-mistress sometimes said. She has her methods, my dear Headmistress.

She was startled when the telephone rang.

"Yes?" she said a little crossly.

Nobody answered and she said, "Who is it?" Then she heard him breathing, levelly and with relish and felt afraid.

"Sarah? Is that Sarah? Sarah, are you listening?"

"Sarah Vincent speaking. Who is it?"

"Sarah. Listen, Sarah. I want you to listen carefully. There's something I want to tell you, Sarah. I love you. I love you very much. I desire you. You know what that means, don't you? I want to come and see you, Sarah. Would you like me to tell you why?" The voice whined and drooled into obscenities.

Her hand shook, with disgust at him and indignation at herself. Then she remembered Justin and drew a deep breath. "Come right on, Lover Boy, I can't wait,' she said firmly and loudly and put down the receiver.

She lifted another essay but the writing was blurred. She was trembling, couldn't control her breathing. How filthy. How ridiculous. Some poor crazed fool. A sickness. It is over now. "That'll choke him off," Justin had said, "that sort hates to be laughed at." Slowly her tension eased.

75

The phone rang again. So Justin had been wrong. She snatched the receiver. "Lover Boy, this is absurd!" she said, using the intonation with which she shattered a riotous Junior Cloakroom.

"I – beg your pardon?"

It was a moment before she recognised the voice.

"George! I'm so sorry."

"Sarah – what in all the earth were you saying just now?"

She shook with laughter as her fright and anger evaporated. She told him what had happened and heard him laughing.

"I thought it was him again, George. I mean, it's very late, isn't it?"

His laughter dried. "I know. I shouldn't ring you as late as this."

"Which is it?" she said maliciously, "Helen or Kitty?"

"Did you see Helen this evening?"

"I had supper with her."

"She wasn't in good form when I called round earlier."

"This was the day Hilary was killed. I suppose you didn't know."

He ignored this and said, "Actually I rang because of Kitty." When he spoke of Kitty all the professional lightness went out of his voice. Unwillingly she asked, "Is there anything I can do? Shall I come round?"

"No. Of course not. It's too late."

"There must be something I can do."

"I don't know. I just don't know."

"How is she?"

"Very restless all day. Very excited. Arguing. This evening she's been shouting. I tried to make her take some of her dope."

The frankness with which he spoke of his wife's condition embarrassed her a little; sometimes she blamed him for using it, sometimes pitied him because he had to use it.

"She ought to take the dope. That's what it's for."

"I can't make her."

"Tell her she must. Tell her I said so. And say if she does I'll come round and see her tomorrow after school, though it isn't my day."

"Would you, Sarah?"

"Of course I will."

"It is very good of you. I don't know why you do this for us." His voice was flat, tired out. She was unwillingly moved by it.

"I couldn't come this afternoon, it was the day we meet for our tea-party. Tell her that, George. And remember to say that they were asking for her. Remember that."

"She'll say she doesn't believe me, that you just said it to please her."

"It's worth taking a chance on."

"I know."

Her power with Kitty pleased her. "You won't last long," George had told her when Kitty had begun to make demands on her, "she uses people, then quarrels with them." She'd lasted a couple of years now. She had learned from George all the rules in the game, absurd devices to outwit Kitty's unhappy agile mind, cheating her to comfort her.

"The key's in the usual place. Thank you, Sarah."

"Shall I tell Helen you rang?" she asked, briskly offensive.

"Don't bother." He didn't intend to rise for that. There was no light in his voice. "Good night, Sarah."

"Good night, George."

CHAPTER SIX

"I was afraid it wasn't awfully good," she said.

"You were quite right, it wasn't."

Sally who had come for the tuition she had missed yesterday sat on the extreme edge of her chair, one leg wound round the other, and wriggled with anticipation as she waited for Daddy Vincent to elaborate. "I did try, really I did, Miss Vincent. But I suppose it was terrible."

She was a fair-skinned ginger-haired child with full cheeks and a thin pointed nose covered with pale freckles, like lentils. She screwed and unscrewed her hands which were pink too and a little glossy, with chewed white-flecked nails. Scold me, her pale eyes entreated. The colourless brows and lashes made her appear distressingly embryonic. Attack, rage, be rough with me, scald me with words, say terrible sarcastic things, worse things than you've ever said to anybody before, so that I can remember them and tell the others and write them down in my diary. Use whips of love on me.

Her essay lay on the table beside the bunch of polyanthus she'd picked surreptitiously from Mum's border. Daddy Vincent could have put them into water but she hadn't bothered and they were flopping already. Outside it was blowy, a bright blue sky with clouds like gigantic swans parading over it. The sun, coming through the window, was hot, shining on the essay, on the limp petals, on her hands, and on Daddy Vincent at her desk just a few feet away who was writing something in the margin.

Her preoccupation gave Sally the chance to look all round the room quickly spying for something to add to her album on Daddy Vincent. You didn't think of Daddy Vincent having a private life, the way other people did. There was a broken packet of chocolate on the mantelpiece and some shoes in the corner. Nothing very special. Probably that door led into the bedroom. You didn't think of Daddy Vincent having a brush and comb and other personal ordinary things like that. You thought of her stalking into class and standing with her feet straddled and the book held out a little in front of her, rocking backwards and forwards ever so slightly, her mouth in a long amused line, ready to come out with one of her famous sarcasms, or looking at you over the top of her glasses in such a way that you knew whatever happened at school was as important to her as it was to you. Or you thought of her laughing, that deep chuckling laugh that Hazel imitated so well.

You didn't think of her as the kind of person who would have Easter cards sent to her. Yet there they were, ranged on the mantelpiece. Pale crosses and lilies and bunny rabbits and pussy willows and Easter bonnets. Easter was a little frightening, not cosy like Christmas. Nobody seemed sure how to celebrate somebody dying especially if, whether you liked it or not, He had died for you. Religion was difficult, like a language that you translated so that it meant something else. You couldn't translate the Crucifixion, or alter it. It was a fact. Some of the things that happened to people in Concentration Camps were just as slow and just as cruel, but those people didn't choose it, the way He had done. And you had to be grateful.

"Was it a frightfully bad essay?" She was still hungry for something more colourful to develop.

Daddy Vincent had finished writing. "It was just very ordinary, not bad, just ordinary. You said the things you thought I expected you to say."

She felt cheated. "Will I have to do it again?" Abuse me, give me a grievance to carry back and wave at them in the cloakroom tomorrow.

"If you think you can improve on it."

79

She got up and sulked across to the window. Daddy Vincent wasn't going to play. It was a pity. Hazel had promised to wait in the bike-shed and now there wouldn't be anything to tell on the way home. "She didn't say *that*?" "She did!" She might even have decided to cry a little. It would be exciting to discover what effect crying would have on Daddy Vincent. But now – "You do create," Hazel would say, "if it wasn't marvellous and it wasn't lousy, what was it?"

Daddy Vincent looked at her watch. "You'll have to run now, Sally, I have an appointment."

She felt her face redden childishly with disappointment.

"But it's only twenty past, Miss Vincent."

"I know. I have to go out."

"Oh, all right!" She put as much cheek into it as she dared, more in fact than she'd intended. Wait for it. Wait for the rockets. This'll be good, Hazel.

"Hadn't you better take this with you?" Daddy Vincent was smiling and holding out her essay. "Read what I've written and do the corrections."

"Will I do another essay for next week?"

"Yes. Choose your own subject."

Choose your own subject. Any old thing, it doesn't matter. I don't really care whether you spread yourself out for me on six pages for next Wednesday or whether you don't. Wednesday at half past three isn't a holy time for me. I don't ache for Wednesdays.

Daddy Vincent put her books firmly together, slid them into a drawer, snapped her biro shut, took off her glasses. Each action was a thread that broke.

Don't do this to me. Don't kill it. Don't let it all fold up. Just let me go on feeling like this about you, that's all. There's got to be something, something absolute, something to start from. If it isn't you it will have to be boys, like it is with the rest of them. I hate boys. I'm frightened of them. Hazel isn't but I am.

"I won't get my exam unless I pass the essay." Panic had made her voice squeaky.

"I know."

She didn't care, she just didn't care.

"But I have to pass. I thought you wanted me to pass."

That was a baby thing to say, she hadn't thought it would sound like that. Daddy Vincent was still smiling. "Wanting won't have any effect on the examiners, will it? Now scuttle."

Once it would have been an affectionate bidding, now it was a kind of insult. She scuttled, contemplated banging the door and then closed it quietly as if someone had died in there. She dawdled down the stairs wasting time, deciding what she would tell Hazel. It must be good. Daddy Vincent stormed. She wept. Daddy Vincent softened, produced a hankie. Something like that. And she would send Daddy Vincent an Easter card, an expensive religious one with a sad text; the signature would be a little blurred.

She idled her way down stair by stair and had reached the hall when Daddy Vincent's door opened and closed again. She was coming already. Rather than be seen still hanging about and have some brisk joke smacked out at her Sally stepped behind the outer hall door which was lying open. Here she could hide and nip out afterwards.

Daddy Vincent was on the last flight. Sally watched. Here she came. What had happened? Where was the glory? The band had stopped playing and all the lights had gone out. She walked that way because her legs were so thick, perhaps they were sore. She had bits of hair hanging down at the back. She looked very ordinary, a bit silly.

She was so occupied in watching Daddy Vincent that she didn't notice the other lady coming up the steps and into the hall. It was the lady who lived on the first floor, all painted up like she always was and her hair brassy, so that you knew at once it was dyed.

"Helen, my dear," Daddy Vincent said softly, "how tired you look."

"Whacked," the lady said, "one of those days, you know."

They stood smiling at each other. It wasn't really Daddy Vincent, it was someone else.

"Poor Helen. I'll look in when I come back, shall I?"

"That would be sweet of you."

"I'd like to." Daddy Vincent's face had gone pink.

The other lady leaned her cheek against Daddy Vincent's and said, "Thank God for Sarah. What would I do without you?" They rubbed cheeks, like cats; two old ladies petting.

"I didn't think you'd be off so soon," the lady said.

"I got rid of my child a little early." They laughed amusedly and Daddy Vincent went off while the other lady climbed the stairs.

Sally felt purged and light, on springs of scorn, when she walked into the bike-shed five minutes later. Hazel had been painting her nails, you could smell the stuff. She was waving them about, waiting for them to dry. "Well, how did the soul-spilling go?"

"Daddy Vincent is a silly old sow," Sally said loudly, not sure if the feeling in her heart was a pain or a pleasure. She did not look at Hazel in case she was grinning.

Hazel screwed up the bottle of polish. "Fancy that now, our Sally has seen the light. I thought we might go home through the park, what do you think? Your Mum won't be home yet."

The park was open and fresh, smelling of newly cut grass. The wind blew her hair back and cooled her cheeks, it was strong enough for her to feel it on her body under her clothes. There were birds moving secretly through the bushes and the ground was pierced with points of orange crocus. "Let's race," Sally said, "Come on – beat you to the trees."

"Be your age."

Hazel was looking towards the far gate where some boys were, four or five of them, sitting on the wall or draped across their bicycles kicking the pedals. They talked noisily and laughed and pretended to punch each other. Show-offs.

The boys had seen them, they were waiting. The sun was shining in Sally's eyes so that even if she narrowed them she couldn't see their faces clearly or be sure which boys they were.

"Come on," Hazel said. They began to walk steadily towards the gate, keeping a swinging pace, almost like dancing. Boys! Oh boy, oh boy! The band had begun to play again, but it was a different tune.

Half an hour later Sarah let herself in at George's hall door and hauled herself up the staircase to Kitty's bedroom. In spite of the fact that her body seemed like a badly assembled collection of breasts and thighs, stomach and shoulders which she carried round with her in clumsy parcels she felt elated, nourished by other peoples' need of her. Life at the moment was rich. That encounter with Helen as she left the house, and Maurice last night – he had not got what he had come for but he had come – and her Charleston pupil – and George – and that silly child with her silly essay. Perhaps she'd been a bit hard on her. And now Kitty was waiting. Gratitude for being so much needed spurred her up the stairs.

This had cooled a little before she reached the landing. She never cared for George and Kitty's house, its lightness, brightness, smooth modern style. So much that was stream-lined and functionally perfect seemed a personal reproach and she felt out of scale. She should have prepared herself more carefully for Kitty who had had all day to sharpen her arguments.

"You're late," Kitty said. She was sitting up in bed stroking the sheet. Her eye measured Sarah. "I've been waiting."

83

Sarah's confidence dwindled further. Already the walls stifled her. She put down her bag and slid out of her coat, trying to find behind this colossal egotism some trace of girl-hood – her most fruitful term of reference – in the tidy, un-pleasant, unhappy lady in the bed.

"And don't throw your coat down like that. You know I hate to see things lying around."

She hung it up, aware that Kitty's eye was not satisfied until the edges of the garment were symmetrical.

It was like a stage sickroom, everything unnaturally cor-rect, equipped for an invalid who didn't use it. A vase of tulips stood stockily, knowing that they gave no pleasure. There was a pile of unread glossies. Untouched grapes. The water jug was full, the glass polished. George provided everything, Kitty refused them all. But he must have per-suaded her to take the dope last night for her eyelids were still heavy with it, lying like hoods on her softly staring eyes.

"Well, how are you, Kitty?"

A bald and stupid opening move. Kitty ignored it, it was obvious how she was. "I suppose the house is looking ter-rible," she said.

Sarah hesitated. Kitty said, "You can either agree with me because it is good for invalids to be humoured, or you can tell me that everything is wonderful and the new woman is a paragon."

"It certainly looks all right to me."

"But you wouldn't know, anyhow."

"Isn't the woman any good?" She had plotted with George to find this latest cleaner and to persuade Kitty to give her a trial. "I thought she seemed very pleasant."

"I don't know. I've never seen her."

"You've – what?"

"I've never seen her her."

"But when she brings you your meals —"

"She doesn't. Don't gape, Sarah. You know I can't stand

strangers. I lock myself in. Every day when George goes I lock my door and I don't unlock it until she's gone."

"Your lunch —"

"George brings it in to me."

"You mean he comes back in the middle of the day?"

"Why not?"

"Isn't it inconvenient for him sometimes?"

Kitty pouted and rubbed her hands through the brown curls that lay thinly across her narrow temples. "I don't know why you come, you just upset me."

"Would you rather I went away?"

"Whatever you like."

I wish I could. I wish I could shout at you and walk out.

"I couldn't have her in here, Sarah. I'd know by the way she looked at me she thought I was mental."

"You shouldn't talk that way."

"You think I'm mental, don't you?"

"No."

"You wouldn't tell me if you did. You're right, I expect. I am. I can prove it. No, listen. You remember the way I looked after this house? The way I worked?"

"You kept it beautifully."

"I did, didn't I? You remember that?"

"I told you I did."

"And now I don't care how it looks any more."

"Because you are ill."

"No. I like to lie here thinking about it getting dustier and dustier, cobwebs and crumbs and grease, and everything cracked and stained and marked with rings where cups have been set down. I don't care."

"You know you don't mean that."

"If I'm not mental I know what I mean. And I must be mental, you see, if I don't care that the house is dirty. It is dirty, isn't it?" She waited slyly to be told that it was.

"It looks all right. I told you that. This room is perfect."

85

"George cleans this room." Kitty smiled. "Sometimes he wears an apron, you should see him."

It was easier when Kitty wept and clung or made extravagant demands or exhausted herself in self-reproach. But last night's sleep had given her strength to use. "You don't try to help me," she scolded when Sarah said nothing. "Now it's your turn to tell me that the only person who can help me is myself."

Sarah said loudly, "We had our tea-party yesterday. Mary was there, and Enid and Florence, and Addie of course, and Joyce. They were asking for news of you."

"Was Helen there?"

"No."

Sarah was conscious of the slow angry hopeless flush that was spreading over her face and down her neck. She turned to the window, looking out to the small overcrowded gardens of this fashionable surburban park, searching for health in grass and sky and leaves. Two gardens down a boy had launched a kite, shouting as it bucked and slewed.

"Put the curtain straight," Kitty said.

"Joyce is having a baby." She tried to put some kind of normality into her voice, "Think of that! We were staggered. They're delighted, of course."

"You've made me miss George's piece on the radio," Kitty said, "it's nearly over now." She turned the switch of the set beside her bed and presently George's voice emerged.

"So you see, there wasn't so very much difference in the end. Perhaps I'm a peculiar sort of fellow, but for me that particular shade of blue has always been – shall we say – significant. I mightn't admit it to everyone and I certainly wouldn't tell everyone why. But there it is!"

There it was, pleasant and easy, a teacups and matinée voice, a voice for sentiment and violins. Superbly done, like all George's broadcasts. A dizzy exhibition of the second-rate.

"So that's that. I've enjoyed telling you about it. It's

sometimes a pleasant exercise, the confessional. And salutary, so they say. Perhaps you'll listen to me next week if it's convenient. I'll be around."

Kitty switched the set off. "I wonder what he tells them about me. I expect they are all very sorry for him."

"I expect they are. And for you."

"They were never my kind of people. Of course he can't give parties any more. He used to give a lot of parties. He's still wildly attractive, wouldn't you say? He never really wanted any children anyhow. The Daddy stuff wouldn't have been in his line, would it?"

A late bread van trundled up the road. Someone was cutting grass. A couple of small girls performed exhibition loops on their bicycles.

"Don't be cross, Sarah," Kitty's voice whined. "I have to talk to someone. You don't know what it's like being this way. I know you think I'm mental."

"I told you what I think."

"If I was mental I could go away to a Hospital somewhere, couldn't I? And everyone would be kind and it wouldn't be my fault any more."

"It isn't your fault."

"Is that what you really think?"

For the first time there was a trace of honesty in Kitty's voice.

"That is what I really think."

Sarah took Kitty's hand. It felt hot and rebellious. They stared at each other defeated by the futility of the game they were playing.

Kitty's hand wriggled free. She straightened the eiderdown where Sarah had rumpled it. "The minister came again last week but I wouldn't see him. I've tried religion. I've tried and tried. It only makes me frightened now, or else I cry."

She will cry soon, that is what we are working for. She will cry and be tired and sleep, over and over and over again.

"I just don't care any more," Kitty said. Her attack was over, soon her private terrors would come creeping up. They sat in silence, listening to the home-coming traffic on the road. Presently George's key turned in the lock, he came up-stairs quickly and stood in the doorway. Sometimes the lion in the Zoo had that regal look, as if at the back of his brain, beyond a world that could be measured by the paces between the bars he still lorded it in forgotten jungles.

"Hallo, my dear. Hallo, Sarah."

Kitty didn't move when he kissed her forehead. He laid a twist of anemones on the bed.

"Nice to see you, Sarah. Have you made yourself some coffee?"

Kitty had unwrapped the flowers. She twirled the bunch between two fingers and pulled out a flower. "Is this your significant shade, George?" Her fingers shredded the petals, and she threw them and the bunch down.

Make a row. Make one hell of a row. What does it matter that she's old and sick and that you loved her once? You can't go on being hit for ever, not time after time.

She had blamed her father for that look of terrible unde-feated patience. "You've tired yourself, dear," George said. He lifted the flowers gently, gathering each scrap of petal, tidying up the mess scrupulously. "Now lie down and rest."

He wiped her fingers clean from the juice, then helped her to lie down, easing her on to the pillows. She didn't speak and offered no protest, didn't look at him. Her eyes were closed. She lay rigid, like a doll. He straightened the sheet across her and tucked it in.

"I expect you're tired too, Sarah."

She had not realised how tired she was. The room swam round her as she rose and she gripped the back of her chair.

"Good-bye, Kitty." Kitty didn't answer.

"I'll bring your things," George said.

She groped her way to the door, fumbling for the handle. He found it first and opened it. When they reached the hall

88

she held her hand out for her coat but he said, "I'll make some coffee, shall I?" and steered her into the lounge. "I'd like some myself."

He knelt to light the gas fire.

"Haven't you had a meal?"

"A sandwich."

"Let me make the coffee."

"You sit there," George smiled. "I expect you make terrible coffee."

There was no sound at all from the bedroom. When he had gone she leaned back watching the fire redden, feeling the warmth on her ankles. She heard him moving about in the kitchen. Presently he came in with a neatly-laid tray. His precision and efficiency hurt her.

"I'll pour out, shall I?"

The coffee was hot and black. She tried to rouse herself. Between us we must collect a little sanity and comfort, enough to behave like rational beings to each other.

"This room's still cold," he said and set his cup down and brought her coat and laid it over her shoulders. She felt devastated by the action and wanted to cry.

"You mustn't look like that, Sarah. It has often been as bad as this before."

"I suppose it has."

"Perhaps we shouldn't ask you to come."

'We' – the dual – 'my wife and I'. The phrase the wedding guests wait for when the bridegroom replies to the toast, the phrase that raises affectionate laughter. The indestructible dual that survives, even if your wife is unhappy and you scheme with your friends to comfort her and find your own comfort with someone else.

"I'll come as long as it does any good."

"Nothing does any good. You have to accept that."

"I don't know that I can," she cried rebelliously. They drank their coffee in silence. Then she put her cup down abruptly. "George – there are women all over the world who

89

are in pain or lonely and forgotten, or desperately poor, or hungry with their children starving round them, or ill-treated or bereaved. And she lies there under her pink eiderdown and makes her own private hell —"

His face flattened defensively. "It is hell. She is very unhappy."

Perhaps it was easier for him to believe she was beyond help. Sarah didn't argue. The fire breathed warmly, spreading orange flowers from the blue points at its centre. He lit a cigarette. She watched the smoke. His hands lay spread on the arms of the chair. There was no sound from upstairs. The need to comfort him grew in her like a pain. She looked at the distance between her hand and his, and was paralysed. Any other woman could have comforted him or at least made some gesture of comfort. She didn't know how. There was one thing perhaps that she could do.

She said, "We didn't turn your programme on in time to hear it all, George, but what we did hear sounded most intriguing."

The light came on in him so promptly that she was shocked.

"It went over quite well, I think." The heaviness had left his face.

"We thought it did."

"Not your sort of stuff, though."

"I don't see why you say that. I enjoyed it."

"Pretty trivial, compared with the kind of work you do."

Her beast sat on the hearth-rug, light from the fire rippled along his mane.

"You obviously create for a market – I don't. But you do it outrageously well, George."

"I'm glad you think so. I kid myself, you know, that there is – well, a little more in it than meets the general ear."

"Oh, there is, there is."

Two beasts now on the hearth-rug. Beast crying unto beast, and a skilful piece of back-scratching.

"I'm sure the technique matters enormously," she said.

"I think the secret is really a sort of implied sympathy. It's easy, when you get the hang of it."

"I dare say, but not everyone can do it."

The skin of his cheek tightened with pleasure. "Well, maybe not."

It was a pleasant game, they played it well. Her turn to serve. "I wonder you don't publish them, George. They'd do well, I'm sure."

"Oh, I don't know," he shrugged. His beast lay on its back, legs in air, scaley stomach exposed to the heat of the fire. She wondered idly how many publishers he'd had his stuff with before he decided to stop trying.

"They'd be bound to lose something on the printed page," she said.

Without warning Kitty began to scream. It was a high-pitched continuous scream like a child waking from a nightmare. Sarah jerked forward. As she watched George rise without hurry and put out his cigarette she knew that he had been waiting for this. He went out of the room and she heard him mount the stairs, heard the door of Kitty's room close. Gradually the screams became less violent. They subsided.

Ten minutes passed. Sarah rose stiffly and put on her coat. The conventionally fashionable room and its furnishings seemed suddenly intimate as if she were a trespasser. She stood in the hall, and at last climbed the stairs and opened the bedroom door.

"I'm going now, George. Good night, Kitty."

Neither of them answered. She didn't think they saw or heard her. He was lying on the bed with Kitty held against him, rocking her in his arms, his light hair against her dark. She looked small, like a child.

"Pretty Kitty," he was saying over and over again. "Pretty, pretty Kitty." His hands moved, caressing her.

Papa was in the hall when she reached Thronehill. She knew at once that this was the day she had returned from her

91

aunt's house in answer to the telegram. Mama was dying again. Sarah had spent yesterday in a train, swaying through wintry countryside, and had spent a sleepless night on the boat forbidding herself to think of what was waiting for her. After the months of absence the house looked smaller. "I am not feeling anything yet," she told herself with private joy as she mounted the steps.

Papa looked smaller too, untidy with grief, trying to make a festival even out of this home-coming. Ellen hovered at the back of the hall; her eyes were red.

"Come in to the warmth, dear. Take the child's coat, Ellen. Did you have a tedious journey? I suppose the boat was packed? When did you eat?"

There was a movement on the stairs. The wooden rings of the curtain that divided the first landing from the corridor leading from it rattled sharply. Someone was standing there, dressed in white. It was a uniformed nurse, but for a moment Sarah thought it was Miss Fennimore. Her room was on that corridor. Papa had seen her looking up, his face was torn with pain, perhaps for a second the whiteness deceived him.

"My daughter's here, nurse."

"I'll tell Mrs. Vincent."

The nurse went into Mama's bedroom with smooth assurance. It was the first time Sarah had seen anyone cross that threshold without any preparation.

Papa gripped her and held her close against him. She hoped he would not feel her body stiffen.

"I'm glad you're here, Sarah."

"How is Mama?"

"She is very ill, dear."

"Shall I go up to her at once?"

"In a minute."

He took her elbows, holding her away from him so that he could look into her face. His eyes with passionate necessity entreated her.

"I need you, child."

"Yes, Papa."

A silent trumpet pealed. I can do it. I can do anything. There is no need to feel. I can make my own terms.

He rocked her gently against him and she yielded to it.

"You must love me – love me," he commanded.

It was easy. The motions and the mask of loving. All right, I'll love you.

CHAPTER SEVEN

"I SIMPLY can't think why ever you asked me to come with you," Addie cried, "I mean – *me*?"

The late afternoon traffic in the centre of the city was building up, and Sarah's mind was on her driving; in any case she had already explained the reasons for her choice to Addie four times over the past ten days, and was now beginning to find it difficult to justify it to herself.

"I told you. They asked me to suggest someone. A three-way interview is easier, so they seem to think."

"But – *me*!"

"We're old friends, you know my work, and you are a writer yourself.

"Not that anyone has noticed."

Addie was wearing rather an absurd hat, like a helmet with bows back and front. There were pink patches on her cheeks and she sat well forward in the car bouncing unnecessarily. The beast, who was in the back seat, breathed warmly down Sarah's neck. "You could have asked Helen."

Not Helen. Writing and loving are two forms of intimacy that do not mix, and Helen's imperceptiveness about her work was a fault that needed to be cunningly by-passed. Addie, who wasn't loved, could make mistakes, could misunderstand, and be forgiven.

"I am torn between terror and exultation," Addie said. "To think that our faces will shine from the corner of every sitting-room in Belfast —"

"They won't. There's horse-racing on the other programme."

"The more selective sitting-rooms," Addie amended.

Sarah found Addie's relish depressing. She had already

94

begun to wish that she had not agreed to this television interview on her work. But the beast, parading, had persuaded her.

"I wonder why they suddenly decided to invite you, Sarah," Addie pursued with brisk unwelcome candour, "it's ages since you've been on, isn't it, and it was always on sound before."

"The bottom of the barrel, obviously. It's a series, they have to keep it going. Is that a new hat, Addie?"

"An old one, I've done things to it. One feels one should make some effort, don't you think?"

Sarah had made none. She wound one of the windows down, declaring that the car was stuffy. "You'll have to take it off, anyway, you know."

"Who do you suppose it will be? A father figure, or one of those beautiful and languid young men?"

"Probably Charles."

"Charles who?"

"I never remember."

Addie clasped her hands. "I think I'd better go home. I'm sorry, Sarah, it was awfully sweet of you to ask me and I do appreciate it, but I am physically incapable of addressing a perfect stranger as Charles. It's not me personally, it's my generation, like butter-knives and calling the lavatory the toilet and eating in the kitchen."

"You needn't say Charles. You can just skip it."

"What is he like in the flesh?"

"Very charming and harmless. We will go in in a cold sweat and come away in a golden glow."

"I don't feel in the mood to be charmed. I wish you hadn't asked me after all. Oh, dear."

Glumly they negotiated the next traffic lights. "I curl up and die," Addie moaned. "Sometimes I feel that people like us have no right to cumber the earth any longer, do you ever feel that way? And yet we've as much right to our three score years and ten as anybody else."

She babbled gently about the fish pie she had left in the

95

oven for Gerald and whether he would remember to turn on the heat at the right time.

"The trouble with us," she said, "is that it is widely assumed that we have Never Really Lived. We've only been born and stayed alive for fifty years and been through two World Wars and the Troubles and seen our country split in two. How much do you remember about the Troubles, Sarah?"

"Coming home from school we had to lie down in the tram because of the shooting, I remember that."

"And we've been bombed of course, and worked our feet to the bone at the Canteen. But we have never been assaulted or ill-used or used violence ourselves or been hungry or lived in a mental institution or a Borstal or been immoral or suffered from perversions other than those induced by our upbringing. I don't see how either of us could be expected to write. Apart from the difficulty of the vocabulary, gentility keeps breaking through."

Sarah laughed and felt better.

"All this about our narrow and restrictive upbringing," Addie went on, "I was happy. I doted on religion. I very nearly saw visions, only that would have been awkward for Daddy, wouldn't it, the Worshipful Brothers wouldn't have liked it. Do you remember how Maurice used to bring his cigarette cards to Sunday School? And I loved my Mother very much, up to the day she died. I'm sure that's psychologically very sinister. And Daddy – well, he was kind but I always knew he was common. Think how much better I'd be writing if he hadn't insisted on making a lady out of me. I used to despise him for being pleased if any of his customers spoke to him at Prize Givings and School Concerts! Your father always did, bless him."

"Oh, dear – here we are." They parked the car and entered the building. A girl at a desk took their names and a lift bore them upwards like votive offerings, feeling faintly sick.

He was a young, pale, faintly troubled man, but he seemed

glad to see them. Thick carpets, arm-chairs, ashtrays and glasses of water lay about for their encouragement.

"We need to establish some kind of a shape," he said, "not that we actually want to rehearse, if you know what I mean. The whole thing is to keep it informal and easy. Forget about the mike, forget about the cameras. You're just here to have a chat. But first we need to find a *shape*."

They discussed a shape with feverish and barren politeness. Sarah wished there was a window somewhere. The beast had gone home. It seemed unlikely that she had ever written a single significant line of poetry. Addie had taken off her hat and it lay on a chair. Her flattened hair reduced her face to a mouse's proportions.

They decided jocularly that they should use each others' Christian name and surname, no prefixes. He was Charles McKenna. Addie became Adelaide Pratt. The idea seemed to depress her.

"And remember we want to keep it light and lively, so come in on each other, take up points that need to be clarified, interrupt me if you want to."

Heavily nervous they agreed and were carried off to the make-up room.

Sarah lay back and resigned her face to a delicious girl in a nylon overall, and carefully ignored the mirror. Addie in the next chair made occasional squeaks. Charles appeared and chatted to the nymph in charge while he ran an electric razor over his cheeks. So that is what a man looks like while he is shaving. Sarah was fascinated. The whole proceedings had taken on an unlikely intimacy. The nymph in nylon left them for a moment.

Addie sat up in her chair, blue-lidded and orange-lipped, her eyebrows unfamiliarly enriched.

"Sarah, you look priceless! Turn round a bit, I want to see you properly. My dear, you are just like one of the Roman Emperors, magnificent and a little debauched, I forget which one it is. I look like a tart, don't tell me!"

They giggled into the mirror at their fantastic reflections.

"Quite happy, I see; well, that's nice!" the nymph said encouragingly, coming back when they didn't expect her, "that's the way it ought to be." They lay back rigid and silent while she dabbed and patted again, and at last she released them.

"Sarah Vincent and her friend and fellow-writer, Adelaide Pratt," the interviewer declared when they were through the sound barrier and the blue monitor screens at which they must not look flickered tantalisingly. "We know Sarah Vincent, of course, for the considerable volume of poetry she has produced very consistently over the past fifteen years or so. Sarah Vincent, perhaps you would tell us a little about how you first commenced to write?"

Sarah Vincent dutifully explained that she had always been interested in writing, had done a little at school, and had found particular pleasure in translating some of the Odes of Horace into English verse. Adelaide Pratt betrayed signs of the liveliest interest and Charles McKenna received the news as if it affected him deeply.

"Horace goes easily into English," Sarah enlarged, "there's an affinity of mood. '*O Fons Bandusiae*'."

"O, really." Charles McKenna leant forward to flick the crease of his trouser leg. "I suppose most of us would regard you largely as a pastoral poet." He misquoted two bad lines from one of her early poems. "Has it been exclusively the Irish landscape that has influenced your work?"

It would be no use telling him of her modest travelling in Europe and Asia since Papa's death. It would take too long, it would spoil the shape. In any case he would assume she had absorbed nothing. His compulsive eye had already reared her in a Belfast drawing-room and sent her to take her holidays in Irish bogland under a Paul Henry cloud.

"I suppose so," she consented humbly.

The saga progressed, growing more and more undistinguished by elaboration. Sarah's confidence ebbed as the young man's glory flowered. Her comments on her work became increasingly banal. "Work in miniature, perhaps one might say," the young man smiled, making it sound like needlework.

This was where the beast should have made his entrance, but there was no sign of him. Beasts in the Province are private animals, secretly cossetted. One requires a licence from London or America to justify a public parade.

Out of the corner of her eye Sarah saw that Addie was restive and therefore dangerous. It was a danger signal she knew. There had been a History mistress once, greenly self-confident and with a thin English voice and a curious opinion of Ireland. Addie did a lot of private homework on the famine and the English atrocities and became very vocal in class. The mistress left after a couple of terms.

"I wonder, Sarah Vincent, whether you might feel that your upbringing and environment here have, so to speak, been a restrictive element in your work?"

The old, old question, the question with which they finally win. Ah, poor young man, for the thin end of a second he had admitted the full flavour of condescension into his voice. These provincial poetesses, these circumspect minds, these canaries pecking lightly at life. As Sarah hesitated Addie fluttered her blue lids and leant forward, becoming suddenly matey and co-operative.

"I think, Sarah, Charles means do we feel ourselves deprived by having had comfortable and happy childhoods and only a literary acquaintance with brothels and dry-closets. Isn't that what you have in mind, Charles?"

Charles began to sweat under his orange powder. "It's an interesting point," Addie went on, "I'm so glad you mentioned it."

"Perhaps, Sarah Vincent – " Charles prompted desperately, but Addie beat him to it.

"Our parents loved us instead of trying to understand us,

it seems one has to choose. Which would you prefer, Charles, to be loved or understood?"

His eyes distended.

"And as for the other," Addie remarked, "I wish you could have seen the Establishment in our house. The size of a drawing-room, twelve feet high, all in pitch-pine and a marble floor. And everything that could be brass was brass. Miles and miles of pipes – full of mystery. One felt like Moses striking water from the rock."

Somewhere at the edge of their stiff eyelids a man in a hairy jersey was rotating his arm as they had been told he would to signal that time was almost up. Gratefully the interviewer expressed thanks to Sarah Vincent and Adelaide Pratt and tied a few random threads of thought in a firm knot.

"If you scold me," Addie said in the car going home – the first time she had spoken, "if you say one single little word I will burst into tears, I'm warning you."

"It was terribly funny, Addie."

"Oh golly, wasn't it?" Addie stretched her feet out, wiggling her toes. "Sarah we can't go straight home after that. Not at once."

They went to an Hotel where sometimes they had attended literary dinners and sat in the Lounge Bar among the homing commercials, nursing gin and lemon and smiling at each other. Addie had put her hat on again, a little crookedly.

"Tell me I was marvellous, Sarah. I was. Just as long as I can make this drink last I was marvellous. If I'd thought of it sooner I could have done it much better."

"If you'd thought of it sooner you wouldn't have had the nerve to do it at all."

"I expect you're right. I wouldn't have missed it for worlds."

"Neither would I. You're washing away your beautiful orange mouth with your gin."

"A fitting end. I think I will wear my eyelids at school to-morrow if I can make them last."

The thought of school crept coldly into the edges of their minds. In defence they drained their glasses and ordered a second gin.

"What about Gerald?"

"He'll be all right. Is Helen expecting you?"

Addie was always curious about Helen, curious and careful. And critical, of course. It was what she didn't say more than what she said. She was only making this straightforward inquiry now because the sudden warmth between them prompted her to admit the relationship. But already a coolness had set in, the evening's lark was nearly over and it grew more difficult every moment to justify it. In any case a florid commercial, across his drink, had noticed Addie and misinterpreted her complexion. Sarah perspired, anticipating what might happen if Addie in her present mood caught his wooing eye.

"Or perhaps George will be calling on her. He comes a lot, doesn't he?"

"A good deal," Sarah said. The glory retreated a little further. "Home, Addie. Come on."

There were school prefect undertones in her voice and Addie rose obediently and took a few moments to straighten her hat and discover whether two gins had done anything to her.

They drove home in silence, separated in mind, each needing privacy to make the difficult transition from one world to the other and unable to compare notes on their progress in case the other had reached a different stage and what was left of sympathy between them snapped at once.

When the car was put away they walked round to the front of the house in silence. The air was cool, but welcome. There was evidence of a moon in the upper sky but the late spring dusk around them seemed dense and deeply blue. Where there should have been shadows under the trees whose branches already were thickened with buds there was pale light from a tide of daffodils that lay like lazy milk. A dowager-breasted wood-pigeon clopped a passage clumsily from one tree to the next.

Sarah lingered on the doorstep, breathing deeply, her large face raised. If she turns poetical on me now, Addie thought, I will not be able to bear it. This kind of beauty still does things to her, Keats and all that. She doesn't have to reconcile it with Gerald and his fish pie and his pills and his dullness and the necessity still to find reasons to love him. Sarah has never tried to translate moonlight into personal relationships and discover how difficult it is. She will go upstairs now and knock on Helen's door and they'll stand at the window looking out at the night in a flush of warm affection and kiss each others' cheeks and say good night and go to bed content. Was it the temperance of love between women that provided spice for it? She felt an indignant and maternal concern for Gerald.

"Good night, Addie."

"Good night."

"It was fun, wasn't it? Charles isn't so bad; it is his office to be superior."

"'Oh Charlie is my darling'," Addie said and turned gladly to her own flat.

She was surprised to hear laughter as she opened the door. Felicity was sitting on the table wearing a pair of those skin-tight pants and dangling scarlet slippers half-on half-off her swinging feet. With a long nail she scraped the crusted edge from what was left of Gerald's fish pie and ate it.

"It's terribly good," she said apologetically when she saw Addie, "we eat out of tins, you know, there's never time for anything else except when Justin decides to do some of his fancy cooking and just now his exams are so close he's given it up. How I hate food, except eating it."

"If I'd known you were coming I'd have left you a little more," Gerald said.

"Greedy, that's what you are."

Gerald curved with pleasure.

102

"I'd better go, I expect he's yelling by now." Felicity scooped herself off the table so that her hair swished audibly across her shoulders. "He generally is. I just came in to borrow some soap-flakes."

"Was he able to give you some?"

"Was I able?" Gerald was flushed, she didn't like the look of him.

The girl smiled childishly – that was clever – and yawned behind her hand. "I'm always sleepy these days, I have been ever since he was born," she apologised and bade them good night.

Addie took her hat off and eased her hair with her finger-tips before she cleared the scattered table. She was tired all at once, perhaps it had been the excitement, the drinks. The pain which she had ignored now pressed insistently as if to make up for lost time.

"Was the fish pie all right?"

"Yes, dear. Nice. Very nice."

She stacked the dishes, not looking at him, waiting for him to tell her what he had thought of the programme. A warm shyness engulfed her. She knew now she had been very silly. When you are middle-aged your dignity is the one thing you must hang on to. When you have a figure like a clothes-horse and legs like a table, when your mind is all old hat and you have forgotten to look if you have a moustache you must still remember to keep your dignity. High spirits are inexcusable. Shame poured over her head and resentment grew in her, thinking of what Helen would be saying to Sarah in the flat upstairs. Soft kind and untrue words, the sort of welcome insincerity you couldn't use with someone you shared a nightly bed with.

She carried the dishes into the kitchen and turned on the water. Her head swam a little. Perhaps she was hungry. She cut a slice of bread and buttered it, cramming it into her mouth, almost too dejected to chew.

She heard Gerald come and stand in the doorway, but she

did not turn. Tell me I made a fool of myself; tell me I was ridiculous. She picked up a dish-cloth, arming herself.

"You certainly surprised me tonight, dear."

"Did I, Gerald?"

"You put him in his place. You fixed him. You knew what you were talking about."

Surprise and resentment hit her a double blow. How stupid he was! Did he really think that? Couldn't he see what had happened? Even if he never reads anything except the papers and detective stories he should have known. You can't be one flesh for all these years without your minds overlapping just a little.

She began to cry and dropped a butter dish.

"Hi, steady on, Booboo."

She mopped her eyes with the dish-cloth and he took it out of her hands as she turned to him.

"Silly girl. Silly sweetheart."

"I'm sorry, Googoo."

"No need."

She hadn't cried so sweetly for years. All her criticism of Gerald and herself, all proper shame melted as he put his arms round her and kicked the broken pieces of china scornfully aside. He produced a handkerchief and she dried her eyes. That was the finish of her eyelids but she did not care.

"What is it all about, anyway?"

"Nothing. Nothing."

She pulled back the curtain behind the sink.

"Look, the moon." She threw the window open.

Moonlight was justified now. It shone with yellow brilliance. It fell on her hands and arms and face, she could imagine there was warmth in it. Twenty-seven years ago there had been a moon like this. She was riding on the back of a motor-bike with her arms clasped tightly round the waist of an assistant from her father's Soft Furnishings, an unsuitable and short-lived romance. She had never forgotten it, had rarely since experienced such strong delight. He smelt of serge and sweat and hair-oil, his body was hard and solid. They consumed mile on mile under the moon, hedges poured back over their shoulders.

"What a moon, Gerald."

"Pretty. Very pretty."

Ah, well. She closed the window. "I'll finish the dishes. You go and sit down, I expect you're tired. I'm glad you weren't lonely, anyhow. She's a nice girl, isn't she?"

"Good legs," he said, "and an elegant bottom."

Sarah tried not to quicken her step as she went up the stairs. If Helen had remembered to watch the television programme she would refer to it casually, as if it were something trivial, something that even if it had gone badly one could not flatter by calling a catastrophe. She would make gentle fun, perhaps, of Sarah the Writer, inviting Sarah to join in. "Schoolmistress Poetess," she would say, quoting from an unfortunate caption in a local gossip paragraph. All right, Sarah would smile, getting a painful pleasure out of it since it was for Helen. Then Helen would be kind and reward her for her humility. This was her habit and sometimes when Sarah needed kindness as she did now it was worth her while to earn it. By an act of mental manipulation she could make her relation to her verses inviolable, a secret thing that couldn't be touched by daily traffic of loves and irritations, and she could return to it when she was ready without apology.

The moon shone through the large window and laid fields of light across the landing. There was a way of walking across this countryside that she had invented in childhood, an act of exorcism of the things that lay beyond the edges of the moonlight, and though she was not conscious that she was doing it, she fulfilled the conditions meticulously.

She knew as soon as she opened Helen's door that George had been there. There was cigarette smoke and the ashtray was littered. Helen was in the kitchen rinsing glasses, an apron round her waist, over her housecoat.

"Come on, come on, you're just in time to be useful."

Her voice was sharp, unnaturally animated, a voice that Sarah knew. The party had ended too soon, and the half-spent mood was to be played out on her.

Helen said, "You're late. Oh, yes, there was this television thing, I'd forgotten; I hope you didn't disgrace yourselves. I expect Addie was pretty terrible, wasn't she? You must tell me all about it. I meant to watch but George was here."

"Actually Addie was rather good." No good explaining and then having to excuse Helen's inability to understand.

"Addie! Oh, very funny! Addie on television!"

Helen laughed in a way that was unbecoming. How much had she had to drink, her colour was high and her eyes had that soft glazed look.

"Have you been taking those pep pills again?"

"You do create. Harry said they were harmless."

Harry had been George's predecessor, a baby-faced doctor fifteen years younger than Helen; his pep pills had helped to close the gap.

The glasses were dried and put away, and they went into the sitting-room where Helen knelt to rouse the fire. Shaded lamps threw small pavilions of light in the room's comfortable elegance. Sarah watched the firelight deepen the colour in Helen's hair.

"All the same I hate you doping."

Helen turned to rise, holding a hand out to Sarah. She stood, holding Sarah's hand between both of hers.

"Dear Sarah, how you fuss." There was a luxuriant slurring in the way she used the words.

Sarah stood rigid, rejecting the caress which was a kind of treachery. Love to her meant an honest mind, something that Helen so often refused, offering instead the easy warmth of skin laid on skin.

"How's Kitty? She's been happier lately. I hope it's going to last."

Helen dropped her hand at once and seated herself on a

106

stool. She slid the heavy sleeves up so that the firelight shone rosily on her arms.

"George didn't say."

"Surely you asked?"

She hadn't intended to sound so sharp.

"Don't bite at me, Sarah. What good does asking do? Do you think George enjoys talking about her? 'Shall we discuss my wife? Our marriage has not been a success, did you know, and now she is a nervous wreck.'"

Sarah flushed, hating the way she sat there, firelit and silky, smiling a little as if she were remembering some joke she had shared with George.

"I didn't mean that – you know I didn't."

Helen shrugged and held out her hands so that her finger-tips became transparent in the firelight. "It's hard to know what you mean sometimes, the way you carry on over Kitty."

"I go to see Kitty because she asks me to, you know that. And I think it helps her a little."

Helen laughed. "I'm sure it does! The fatally compulsive Sarah. You were always like that, even at school – the Leader of the Bluebell Patrol and all the ardent little Bluebells! Have you forgotten? I suppose it's a natural law of compensation or something clever that has a name. God how funny we looked in our uniforms!"

Sarah said, "Are you trying to be bitchy, or have you had a lot to drink?"

"Quite a lot. But hasn't it ever struck you, dear Sarah, that George is the person who ought to be giving Kitty whatever it is that she's getting from you?"

Angrily she said, "And Kitty who should be giving George whatever it is he comes here for."

Helen raised her brows and said amusedly, "You've never been able to decide whether I go to bed with George, have you?"

All her skill in anger drained away, leaving her cold and

shaken. How successfully Helen turned it into a joke against her.

"It is no concern of mine," she said. This was true, she had carefully avoided being concerned. Perhaps they were lovers, perhaps not. Easiest not to speculate. She had observed the love affair incuriously and had avoided guessing at its nature and degree. In this way she could also avoid any comparison between George's love for Helen and her own.

She went and stood at the window staring out into the garden now a mosaic of moonlight and shade. The floral urns, lurching a little with age, grass-grown and whiskered, peopled the lawn with unlikely shadows.

"You imagine us rolling about on the bed, don't you, Sarah? You do, of course. I don't suppose you imagine very accurately but you do your best."

"Helen —" She took a step towards her, but Helen had risen and moved away while violent and angry tears poured down her distorted face.

"Shut up – do you hear! Go away! What do you know about it anyway? You, that never needed it, the intelligent woman. You should have married Hubert, you'd have been a good pair. He wouldn't have had to apologise to you for all the times he couldn't —"

"Stop! Stop!"

She seized Helen's arms holding them tightly to try to control the shaking that jerked the words from her body.

"That was what Hubert was like, didn't you know? Large and blonde and gentle. The unreliable lover. I don't wonder Elspeth couldn't stick it! She's left him, did I tell you? I wonder she stuck it so long!"

Helen began to laugh, a high-pitched titter. Sarah hit her, one cheek and then the other. The laughter dried at once and after a moment's silence was replaced by noisy unrestrained crying. Sarah held her, feeling no pity at all, just a numb relief that it was over.

"Sarah! Sarah!" Helen wept.

"You're all right," she said idiotically over and over again. "You're all right, Helen. It's over now, you're all right."

She was glad when Helen allowed her to steer her into the bedroom. She lay down on the bed. Sarah pulled the cover over her and she didn't move.

"You'll be all right now," Sarah said, and turned and left her, without looking back.

Helen lay on her back staring at the ceiling and did not move. None of this would have happened if it had not been the spring. Next week it will be May. I cannot bear the spring. The aching blossoming spring. Lilacs and laburnums hanging heavy out over garden hedges so that suburban pavements are scattered with petals and the air all scented and young girls in pale frocks with bare tender arms, laughing together. The empty enchanted evenings, stretching your body like pain. What can you do to defend yourself?

I didn't intend to tell Sarah that Elspeth had left Hubert – or to tell George. I only told him because he was so preoccupied this evening, not playing my game, and I needed it. So I thought – something's got to happen here, we'll have an explosion, see what that does. Tell him about Hubert. It's nearly over between George and me. I have to hang on to him because there is no one else. There is the unthinkable thought that George could be the last. It isn't true, it couldn't be. But George and I have enjoyed ourselves, he knows the rules and he is very sweet.

So I said, "The woman my husband has been living with has walked out on him. What do you think of that – just up and gone!" And his face became tender and concerned at once – oh, automatically, it was wonderful – and he said, "Oh, my dear," with that look that still makes my heart turn over and always will every time I remember it, and he ran his hands up the sleeves of my housecoat into my inner elbow where the blue veins are. "Oh, my dear."

And I said, "What do you suppose a proper wife's proper reactions are to a thing like that, George? Or am I a proper wife, I'm a bit at sea. What is one expected to feel when one's husband's mistress packs up and goes?" I was watching his face, taking my light from him like I always do. It is the only way. George always gives me light, I've never had to ask for it. That's one of the things I need from a man. Honesty isn't any good, I tried it with Hubert. I was young, it hurt too much. I learned how to play this game with Oliver. Perhaps if I'd gone to bed with him I wouldn't have to go on playing it with every man afterwards. Then he moved his hands against my breasts, holding them there though he knows what that does to me. "What happens now, George?" And he said (and I wish I could remember the tone of his voice), "I suppose, my dear, that now you will have to consider whether or not you will go back to him." And then I moved away to pour him another drink so that he couldn't see my face, and I said, "Supposing he doesn't want me?" and he didn't answer, and I had another drink myself.

George wouldn't have suggested that there was a possibility that I'd ever go back to Hubert if he cared about losing me. Or perhaps he could afford to say it because he was so sure of me; that would be nice to think but I know it isn't true. And now I've bitched Sarah. Not that I mind. Not Sarah. She'll come back if I want her. I might want her if there is nobody else. And there is nobody else because my daughter was killed when she was a little girl and Hubert never gave me another child.

Later she rose and tidied the bed and washed her face and made coffee and drank it, doing everything with careful precision like someone who is preparing for a journey, and then set out her sleeping-pills beside the pillow and before she took them picked up the telephone and asked the operator for a trunk call.

While she waited for the connection she heard the tele-phone in Sarah's flat ring four times before it was answered.

"Yes?" Sarah said.

"Sarah? George speaking."

"Oh, yes, George."

"Sorry to ring you as late as this."

"That's all right; I was working."

"Still working?"

"Pre-exam tests, you know what it is."

"I can guess. Sarah, are you all right?"

"Yes, of course."

"Your voice sounds odd, I wondered. You haven't been getting any more of those dirty phone calls, have you?"

"No. The treatment worked."

"Sarah – I was in with Helen this evening."

"Yes, she told me."

"You've seen her then?"

"I called in."

"Was she all right? Did she seem upset or anything?"

There comes a point where loyalties and expediencies dis-solve and only the truth will do.

"I thought she'd been drinking too much."

George didn't answer, and Sarah said, "She gets depressed sometimes. I wouldn't worry. She'll be sleeping now. How is Kitty today?"

"Very much the same."

"Tell her I'll be round to visit her tomorrow."

"She'll look forward to that."

"I don't know if she will, but I'll come."

He said, "Thank you," humbly in a voice she didn't recognise.

"No need."

"You sound tired, Sarah."

"My dear George," she snapped. "don't add me to your list of responsibilities."

She hung up before he could answer. 'You sound tired.'

It used to be an oblique form of criticism. You are not at your best, you have missed a trick, you are tired. Now that we are older it has become a term of affection. 'You sound tired, dear.' That easy self-generating warmth, emotional rhubarb, the herb of generosity.

CHAPTER EIGHT

THE fear by this time stretched out in front of her like a shadow, constant and inescapable, and life had become so terrible that it was unreal. This unreality was an extra reason for panic. Everything was cardboard except what was going on inside her body and inside her mind. People were cardboard. Only sometimes when they laughed, or pausing seemed to stare at her, cardboard grew menacing, became real, cardboard was the only authentic and proper substance, and it was she who was the oddity, the freak, the outcast.

It was a hot afternoon in June, close and airless, and sun shone unremittingly through the large windows of Daddy Vincent's room. Sally's head swam and ached and the sunlight mocked her. The fact that this was the last of Daddy Vincent's Discussion Groups before the exams began was a lesser, though at the moment a more immediate reason for uneasiness.

The most monstrous thing about being afraid all the time is the way it can go on and on long after you have decided you can't bear it any longer. There is no way of stopping, and nobody seems to notice. I am terrified how well I can pretend. I feel as if it was spelt out in big letters right across my face. Even Hazel hasn't noticed. She never misses much and it is frightening that she is missing this. She is filing her nails quietly round the side of her chair, blowing on them like she wouldn't dare to do if this was a proper class, daring Daddy Vincent to tick her off. Daddy Vincent hasn't noticed either, but that isn't surprising because it isn't the sort of thing she would notice anyway. But Mum – that frightens me more than anything. I have got into the way of turning my mind to stone rather than think what it will be like when she does find out, but it seems impossible that I have spent twenty-five – twenty-six nearly – days with this fear shut up inside me, and that Mum doesn't know anything about it.

Last Friday I was doing my prep in the kitchen when she came in with a pile of parcels, the way she always does on Fridays the day she gets her money. She was wearing a new blouse and she said, "I've got a present for you, Sal," and I said, "Oh, have you?" and she said, "What's up? You're looking peaky – having a bad day or something, love?" and I said something smart and ran up to my room before she could catch me with her love and her present. She called, "What are you doing up there?" And I said, "Nothing," pretending to be busy, opening drawers and banging about, making a noise to protect myself with until I was ready to come down.

Every night I think it'll be all right in the morning, and when I wake up and it isn't, I think it'll be all right by the time I go to bed tonight, but it isn't, and now I am trying not to think this any more because being disappointed makes me feel sick and if I feel sick it means that what I am afraid of is true.

Daddy Vincent is talking about Lord Byron. We are supposed to be discussing love poetry, ha ha, but it is hot and anybody who knows any love poetry has talked about it, very wet some of it was, and now Daddy Vincent is doing the talking. There are only eight of us here, we've dwindled this term. There was terrific competition to be one of Daddy Vincent's Chosen Twelve at the beginning of the year and everybody was keen. "It isn't school," she said, "just a chance to get together and I talk about the sort of things that interest us, and twelve's a reasonable number."

People did talk at the beginning – about freedom and the H.P. and mixed marriages and the Bomb, things like that. There was tea and cakes and we washed up afterwards. We gave Daddy Vincent a fountain-pen at the end of the Christ-

114

mas term, and bath salts at Easter, and each time she was surprised, and her face grew shiny and solemn while somebody made a speech thanking her, and I hoped she would know it was my idea, and that I was the one who collected the money and organized it all.

In ten minutes from now Daddy Vincent will close her book and wish us good luck in our exams and say that she's enjoyed the discussions and she hopes we have. And then she'll get up and go to the door, ready to shake hands with each of us, like she always does on the last meeting in the term, as if she didn't expect any present, keeping her surprise very well hidden until somebody starts to make a speech. Only this time she'll need to hide it extra well, because she isn't getting anything.

It was me, I suppose. I didn't bother on purpose. Some of them said, "What about the presentation, Sal?" and I said, "Oh, do you think we ought to bother?" and in the end nobody did. I was glad, because it was really Daddy Vincent's fault that what has happened to me did happen.

There's a picture of Lord Byron in the book, she's passed it round. Real smooth and very sexy, Hazel says. He is rather like the boy I met in Daddy Vincent's flat once, Justin, I always hoped I'd meet him again. Perhaps if it had been someone like Lord Byron or Justin I would have felt different. I know I ought to have felt different, or else why do people create about it like they do, and die for it, and poets write poetry about it. But if that's what they mean by bliss, then I've had it – with Jim Riddle under the laurel bushes at the back of the park.

Jim was the only one who hadn't got a steady so he was the one I got. "We're the left-overs," he said. He was quite funny sometimes, we used to laugh a lot. He was taller than me even when I was wearing my high heels. "Fancy! Sally!" they said at school. Hazel was going with Don by this time. "Watch it, kid," she'd say when they left me and Jim by ourselves, and we used to kill ourselves laughing at her. He wasn't romantic I suppose but I felt more comfortable with him, being the funny kind. I expect I liked him in a sort of way, not passionate but the books say you don't expect that right away. His hands were very cold always. But I was glad I had a boy. "You're not normal, there's something wrong with you," they used to say at school. Well, I was normal now.

It was a beautiful film, full of love and passion and long long kisses with their mouths open. I felt light and happy walking home. I couldn't see Jim very well because it was getting dark. He bought ice-creams instead of chips and I was glad because it was warm, the first warm evening this summer. Jim wasn't as funny as he generally was. "You're all right," he said, "do you know something, Sally, you're all right." And we walked home slowly, taking long swinging steps with my head on his shoulder, watching how the street lights as we passed them threw out one long shadow for the two of us on the pavement in front. It was the first evening I'd been out just in a dress and the tops of my arms were cold.

We came beyond the shops, away from the neon lights, and we were passing the park which was all closed up when Jim said, "Bet you you wouldn't dare shin up the railings and go inside," and I said, "Bet you I would." That was the way I was feeling, light and lovely. And I climbed up, hitching my skirt up high round my legs to avoid the spikes. I must have looked a sight and Jim laughed. I knew he was staring and I didn't care, just stood there, pulling my skirt up higher. And both my stockings whanged into ladders and I felt them trickling down my legs. I laughed and jumped down on to grass on the other side. And Jim jumped down after me.

All the time there was something singing right through me, and I thought, well this is bliss, this is rapture, it has to happen sometime and I'd just as soon it was Jim.

It was very dark and private in the park, quiet and empty except for pieces of paper blowing about. And I waited for Jim to say something but he didn't. He grabbed hold of me

116

and pulled me in behind the laurel bushes. And all of a sudden the singing stopped and there was nothing I wanted so much as to get away from him, and I tried to run but he held on to me and my dress tore.

"You shut up," he said. "Shut up or I'll fix you. What did you think you were coming in here for anyway?" So it was no good and after that I made myself dead, not even fighting any more or hitting him. It was easiest to be dead. Even then, looking up at the sky through the laurel leaves I thought something could happen for me, that the stars could explode or something, but nothing did and he hurt me. And all the time the cars were going past on the road and it began to rain on to my face.

I climbed back over the railings by myself after he'd gone and got upstairs without Mum hearing me because she was rowing with Dad. But next day I told Hazel that she'd caught me and that I had to be in early for a month, to stop her asking questions. I saw Jim once across the street when Mum sent me for a message. He was walking with a string of boys. He looked away at once, but I knew by his face that he was scared.

I am twenty-six days over the time now, and sometimes I run upstairs and look at myself but there isn't anything to tell me I'm any different from what I was before it happened. My head aches most of the time but that is the worry. It is like being caught in a trap that is inside you, so that you can't get away.

> 'So we'll go no more a-roving,
> So late into the night.'

You bet we won't. Not now. Not when we know. But when she reads it like that there is a terrible kind of sadness in her voice and the words are beautiful, and they make you think that poetry could be true even if the thing is a swindle. Or did the poets just think it all up? Anyhow, it doesn't matter now or alter things.

'Though the heart be still as loving,
And the moon be still as bright.'

But I wish so many people hadn't told so many lies. I mean, if that's all there is.

The sun went out like a light and rain drummed on the window. "That's all," Miss Vincent said, and she closed the book and looked round smiling. "And time's up, so this is the end of our Discussion Group. I've enjoyed it, and I think you have. And now I just want to wish you good luck in your exams."

She moved to the door and opened it, preparing for the hand-shaking ritual. This was always a solemn moment. It was the moment too when the presentation speech ought to begin, catching Daddy Vincent with her hand on the door-knob, turning round to face them, looking pleased and sur- prised, dignified and shy at the same time, an unusual Daddy Vincent for whom in previous terms they had felt a surpris- ing affection.

No one spoke and there was a self-conscious silence which the girls hurried to break by filing out. Some of them were pushing.

"Good-bye, Celia."

"Good-bye, Miss Vincent; thank you, Miss Vincent."

They shook her hand emphatically and avoided looking at her face.

"Good-bye, Veronica, and remember – don't work too hard."

This was always a joke but today the laughter was thin.

"No, Miss Vincent; good-bye, Miss Vincent."

They remembered the cream cakes and the tea and the fun they had had over the washing up, and the times they had been surprised at the wisdom and wit of some of the things they had heard themselves saying. Let's get out of here – quick.

Sally was the last to go. She had hung back, wanting to be the last, wanting to make sure that Daddy Vincent had been hurt. There was no sign yet. It seemed unfair that an adult should be able to get away with it like this. There must be some way of establishing that the insult had been deliberate. She offered her hand, staring into Miss Vincent's face.

"Good-bye, Sally."

"Good-bye, Miss Vincent."

Had it come off? She wasn't sure. Daddy Vincent was still smiling with kindness which was unbearable. How could she smile like that? But for a moment her eyes seemed to dull. It was happening! She understands. She has been hurt. I think she has been hurt.

There wasn't time to find out. A man had appeared on the landing and stood, straightening his buttonhole while Sally, bleak with anger, watched Miss Vincent withdraw her hand and turn to the man, her face lightening.

"So sorry, Sarah, I didn't know you were busy."

"The girls are just going."

The man smiled at Sally as she passed him. She'd seen him on the tele quite often. So his hair was white. You'd think on the tele it was blonde. "Sexy at his age, what do you know?" Hazel had maintained. She always said it was white.

The door closed and Sally came downstairs. Daddy Vincent, looking at a man like that! Was it just because he's got her out of a hole? It was more than that. Daddy Vincent! The person I used to be cracked about when I was a kid, the old god that I kick around. Poor silly thing. Poetry coming out of her ears and her big shiny face looking at a man like that!

The others had gone on when she reached the hall door. Sally was half-way down the drive when suddenly she halted, recalled to her former wretchedness which for a moment she had forgotten, coming back into the old prison as a jolt of sickness ran through her body. Was it sickness?

Don't stop. Don't stop or hope. It is no good hoping. I have hoped too often. Nothing has changed, nothing is different. I had forgotten for a moment, that was all, and it is dangerous to forget. I will walk down the avenue, holding myself very steady, looking at the garden and noticing things that are outside myself.

The rain is over but the pebbles on the drive are still dark with it and there is a smell of leaves and grass. It must have been a beautiful garden once. Everything is overgrown and tangled now. There is a lilac tree fallen sideways because the blossoms on it are so heavy. There is a big straggling bush with flowers on it like plates of cream. Two thrushes are arguing, floundering about in seeded lupins. Sometimes you can see them, sometimes you can only hear them. The rain has washed the petals off the rhododendron so that the white points are bare and the flowers are lying on the ground like a red stain. And high up, much higher than you would expect it, there is a spray of pink roses. We had hoops of pink roses like that once at the dancing class —

She stopped, swaying with dizziness, and took a few steps into the uncut grass that grew high at the side of the drive, and lay down in it and held her body and rocked backwards and forwards and wept and laughed, and then twisting round laid her face down among the wet grasses, rubbing against them. Finally she rolled over, staring at the sky.

I have a pain. I have a pain. Glory Be and Hallelujah! This is bliss. This is rapture. I have a pain.

CHAPTER NINE

"Come in, George," she said, "I'm glad to see you."

The words were unnecessary, her welcome she felt sure must exude visibly from her. She felt a theatrical desire to kneel down and clasp George round the knees, uttering a Shakespearean phrase. No one could have arrived more opportunely. She had disciplined herself with pleasant anticipation to be surprised by the presentation and to enjoy the emotional formality with her girls, and she was quite unprepared for what had happened. It was unreasonable to be hurt like this, as much as this. The sight of George, standing on the landing saved her from making a fool of herself in front of the child and she was now prepared in gratitude to make all sorts of a fool of herself in front of him.

Sanity prevailed and she beamed at him foolishly.

"Sit down, George."

She waved a hand at the crumpled cushions in the disordered chairs, aware suddenly of the room's shortcomings and that the air smelt like a class-room.

George went to the window and stood swinging the blind cord. She noticed that for once he did not seem to be watching himself in the driving mirror.

"Kitty," she diagnosed. "Is something the matter? How is she?"

He missed the cord as it came back to him and let it go on swinging in diminishing journeys.

"The heat always upsets her."

"She told me you were getting an electric fan."

"I did, but she's worried by the noise it makes." He turned to look at her as he said this, defying her to criticise Kitty's contrariness, his last remaining kind of loyalty – 'my wife and I, reasonable people both, we do not care for the noise of the electric fan.'

"Perhaps if I had a word with her –"

He hit the cord so that it rattled against the glass where his breath had misted it and then said, "I'm looking for Helen. Do you know where she is?"

His words like cold water had an invigorating effect on her temper and she snapped, "I haven't an idea – I'm not Helen's keeper, you know."

He stared, she thought for a moment he was going to laugh.

"What is it, Sarah? Is something the matter?"

She shook out cushions vigorously, making an occupation of it. Cascades of crumbs fell over the carpet.

"Nothing." What a fool, won't you ever learn? Mixed pastries and love poetry with the Lower Fifth, why do you *do* things like that, or if you must do them, why do you let them matter so much?

"Helen generally phones or leaves a message," he grumbled, "and Addie isn't in either."

It was unusual for him to discuss the mechanics of his friendship with Helen. He came and went smoothly and silently as if the relationship were regularised by the ease with which it was maintained.

"Addie has gone to the tea-party; this is the day."

George brightened. "The tea-party – Helen forgot to tell me."

"I don't know. Helen hasn't been to one for a long time."

"But she goes sometimes."

"Sometimes."

He stirred the crumbs on the carpet with his shoe and asked without looking at her, "Is Helen all right? Do you think she's worried about something? She has seemed a little – detached recently, don't you think?"

"I don't know what you mean," she lied.

"You must have noticed. She confides in you more than in anyone."

This tribute was unusual; she filed it for future reference and gave him the reasons which she given herself to account for the change in Helen. "This is her busy season. Scores of weddings. She never has a moment."

"Then you don't think there's anything the matter?"

"I don't think so."

George said, "She is so much alone," with such bogus emphasis that she felt he was trying to establish the fact for himself and not quite succeeded.

"Except for you and me and dozens of friends and her absentee husband."

The shocked expression on George's face pleased her. She felt a little sorry for him and said, "I think perhaps she's tired. I know she is planning to get away for a little break next week."

"Do you know where she is going?"

She had hoped to have this information from him and in her disappointment she snapped, "Ask her, why don't you?"

He didn't answer. Suspicion dawned slowly. Helen had told him, too. From the little silver-framed photograph that she kept on her mantelpiece of Helen coming out of the Church on her wedding day, Hubert, gay, blond and noble, leaned out menacing them. Both wearing buttonholes, Helen's badge.

"What about the summer?" George said, elaborately casual. "What is she doing then, do you know? I mean apart from your ritual fortnight at the seaside – that arrangement holds, I'm sure."

His voice made fun of it. Girls together, the ritual fortnight, supervising the rise and fall of the waves.

"I expect so."

"You've booked?"

Of course Helen had booked, she always did it, and she had been so busy she hadn't mentioned it. It was a foregone conclusion, like a favourite gramophone record, there was nothing they needed to discuss. The mixture as before, the bedroom looking out over the garden's clipped hedges to the sea, the table in the second bay window, their special corner in the lounge, features as permanent as the beach, the pier, the ruined castle that was somebody's Folly set on the mound overlooking the village street. Helen hadn't mentioned it and neither had Sarah because perhaps even to discuss it might suggest there was a reason why this summer shouldn't follow the pattern of all the previous summers.

"So you haven't booked," George decided.

"Why you should come charging in on me like this when I'm taking a class, catechising me —"

He had got what he'd come for, could afford to be humble. "I'm sorry, Sarah. I didn't know you had a class."

Vulnerable as always to even the smell of kindness she said. "It was only my Discussion Group, our last meeting before the end of term."

He smiled. "Ah, yes, I've heard about that. Is this the meeting where they embarrass you by making a flowery speech and a presentation?"

She caught the blind cord and discarded it, remembering his use of it. "There was no speech this time, and no presentation either."

"The little bitches," he said softly. "Why?"

You are too quick for a man, too perceptive.

"I haven't an idea," she barked, "perhaps you'd like to suggest one."

He looked at her with disapproval. She remembered that when she was a child and in distress once the decision to cry had been taken she allowed herself to be swept along in a tide of luxuriant sorrow, yell on yell, until her nurse directed calmly, "Go and look at yourself in the glass, Miss Sarah," where the sight of her red face, open mouth and streaming eyes frightened her into some kind of self-control. George's expression suggested that a look in the glass would steady her up.

"You'd better go, George."

"Sarah —"

"Please go."

"They are only a pack of silly children, you know that."

She wanted to contradict him but any phrase she could have used would have sounded extravagant or silly – 'they are my heart, my breath's nurselings' – and so she said, "There's Helen's car now. She must be home."

She didn't blame him for leaving her so eagerly or for the lightness of his voice greeting Helen over the bannisters. But she went to the window and threw up the sash, welcoming the garden and the excellence of things as opposed to people.

High June, no better season. The lime trees were ponderous already but still deeply green, their broad leaves breathing vapour after the rain. The sunlight, unnaturally strong for late afternoon fell heavy and solid on the overgrown shrubberies where bush competed against bush with a triumphant flourish of blossom on the winning spray. Mr. Boyd's nephew had cut the lawn last week, arriving in a glossy sports car, and had left the edges unclipped so that they lay like the fringes of Roman Emperors over the weedy paths. The grass had a chewed appearance, rough and discoloured, the mowing had been a battle. Felicity had left a nappy and a magazine on the garden seat, and a cup but no saucer. Gerald's deck-chair was empty but his hat pinned his newspaper to the ground beside it. Felicity's baby waved stout naked legs from the pram. The place had the tattered appearance of a public park near closing time.

Sarah closed her eyes, hungry for ghosts, for the lawn striped in two shades of green from Mr. Boyd's precise and frequent attentions, for the smack of croquet balls, for the sight of Ellen in black with starched trimmings carrying a well-appointed tea-tray.

The child in the pram wailed and Felicity appeared, slip-slopping over the grass in mules; she was wearing black pants and a scarlet bra. She scooped her son up and sliding a strap off her shoulder offered the boy her breast, standing. When he had sucked a moment and fallen asleep she put him back on his pillow and found a handkerchief with which to wipe her milk from the corner of his mouth. Looking up she saw Sarah watching from the window and waved as she wriggled her breast back into place. Sarah waved back, mesmerised by the operation and Felicity's skill. She had never seen a child suckled before. Even with extra coaching Felicity two years ago hadn't been able to grasp the most elementary points of Latin construction.

Addie knocked and came in wearing her hat and coat, like a fully-rigged maypole. She looked strained, her eyes competed for kindness.

"I thought you'd like to hear about the tea-party but send me away if you don't."

Sarah was glad of the diversion. "Addie, are you all right? You don't look well."

Addie ignored this. "I suppose Helen will give you all the news anyway; did you know she honoured us with her presence today? Oh, very friendly. As if it wasn't the first time she'd bothered to come for months and months, and everyone was so delighted to see her. What is it about Helen? Charm, I suppose. Oh, all right, I'm getting the message, but nobody except Helen could waltz in like that and pick up all the threads before she'd taken her gloves off. Has anything happened between her and George – I mean, is it cooling off a little?"

"George was looking for her, he's there now."

"Tell me to go to hell, dear, I just wondered. I noticed he hadn't been in and out as much as usual. Those sort of ornamental affairs can go on indefinitely, but I think the end is in sight. It must be rather frightening, I mean there's bound to be one that'll be the last."

"Tell me about the tea-party," Sarah said firmly. "Who else was there?"

"Pamela, my dear, home on furlough. It was frightful, she asked a blessing over the crumpets. We all froze."

"There's no reason why she shouldn't. It's a Christian country."

"There was an accusing tone about it, I thought it was anti-social, and it made us all most uncomfortable. And yet I don't know why – we all grew up with it."

Papa asked a blessing before every meal, breaking off in the middle of a conversation as though prompted by his gastric juices, and assuming in his role as worshipper a kind of godhead. Miss Fennimore's lashes fluttered as her lids closed and she enjoyed bending her head when his hand was lifted. Grace in latter years always included a blessing invoked, 'on her Thine handmaid on whom Thou has seen fit to lay the heavy hand of affliction.' After the Amen Papa carved and Miss Fennimore carried Mama's tray up to her bedroom.

"Who else was there? Florence?"

"A little dimmed by Pamela today, poor dear. Charity Bazaars can't compete with the Mission Field. Sarah, I love them all, why do I talk like this? And Mary. She has found a new man for her feet, a wizard, she says we must all go. And Joyce, of course."

"How is Joyce?"

"Monumental already, do you think it could be twins? Maurice called to drive her home, enormously attentive, as if he were taking delivery of a crate or something. Personally I think he's terrified. He's getting very gravy-stained is Maurice; someone ought to do something about it. It was in between Rose and Joyce that he went like that. I think it's a kind of pose now, University types tend to go to one extreme or the other."

"He was always a bit messy even in his sailor suits."

Addie had wandered to the window. "There's Gerald out in the garden again. He shouldn't sit around, there may be mosquitoes. It's that girl, she makes him restless, poor dear. I think he's working up to something."

Addie made for a chair and sat down rather suddenly.

"Addie, what is it?"

"Just the weather. I don't know. Sometimes on summer evenings I get plain melancholy for no special reason."

It was depressing to see Addie deflated.

"Tell me more about the party."

"No more to tell. How did the presentation go?"

"There wasn't any."

Addie stared. "Oh, Sarah. Why do things matter so much? And they get smaller and smaller."

Unexpectedly Addie began to cry.

"Addie, dear —"

"Don't be kind, please. It's Helen with you, it has always been Helen, don't tell me. I just hover around picking up little bits along the edges. What is it about you, Sarah? You'd have been a wow in a nunnery, do you know that?"

She opened her handbag and collected a handkerchief and blew her nose. A fearful embarrassment locked them in silence. A letter fell out of Addie's bag and Sarah picked it up and gave it to her.

"A letter from Alistair. He writes every week, doesn't he? What's his news?"

"I haven't read it."

"Surely —"

"It is either hot or wet, Alistair is either well or a little under the weather, business is either brisk or dull, the news in the papers is either disturbing or encouraging, and he hopes we are both keeping reasonably well considering – considering what, I wonder – and not overdoing things."

"Oh, Addie —"

"You can read it and see." She held out the envelope. Sarah waved it away, mumbling "I'm sorry. I'm sorry."

The sunlight went out and the room darkened as rain fell again. It fell in long straight silver wires, not hitting the window pane but producing from trees and shrubs a sound like distant applause.

"I must go and see about Gerald."

"Why don't you and Alistair get on? What is the difficulty?"

"It isn't that we don't get on. I committed the unforgiveable sin of being at the other end of his umbilical cord, that's all," Addie said and bustled out of the room, quickening her descent of the stairs at the thought of Gerald's poor shoulders out there in the needling rain, and glad of this spur to her compassion.

CHAPTER TEN

"Hips?" the saleswoman inquired with the air of a Father Confessor to whom all things are credible and who finds himself concerned but no longer outraged by life's irregularities.

"I beg your pardon?"

The woman shifted the weight of her tired habitual elegance from one foot to the other and repeated, "Madam's hips?"

"I am not sure," Sarah stammered, embarrassed to a point of wild confusion. It was a mistake, it must be a mistake, she was amazed to have placed herself in a position where her hips were a matter of public concern, and could hardly remember what had prompted her to come.

The women's professional eye slid round her like a snake and drawing tight decided "Forty-eight – well, we have a few gowns we could show you —"

"It was the olive green one in the window, the one with the sort of silky bow —" Like a child at the bottom of a Christmas Tree.

"Thirty-six, dear," the saleswoman said tolerantly, "a sweet gown, but no good for madam."

Sarah felt as if her proportions, already remarkable, were increasing minute by minute and would soon fill the space between the glass counters of this smart shop. Alice felt like this in the house of the White Rabbit, a mass of swelling thrusting flesh. She tried to summon her practised weapons of intelligence and authority against this woman. I will not be bullied, I am the customer, I am always right, but the woman's eyes slid off her as soon as she had finished speaking as if the situation were so obviously hopeless that the last word was hardly worth claiming.

"You must have something," Sarah muttered.

"Miss McLoughlin – a moment, please!"

A second saleswoman tucked her pencil in at the back of her ear and joined them.

"Miss McLoughlin, have we anything in a gown that would suit Madam?"

"An afternoon gown?"

"It is an afternoon gown?"

"I expect so." There was probably a funny side to this, but at the moment she could not lay hands on it. "I don't propose to cook the breakfast in it."

The women raised their eyebrows slightly and lowering them again scrutinised her, pursing lacquered mouths. The last remark had been a mistake. I am a piece of meat on a hook, I am an offence against womanhood, a freak, a monster, I have no right to the cubic feet of perfumed space I occupy here, let alone to an attempt at humour. I will go away and find a roomy tent and live in it, in decent shapeless obscurity.

The saleswomen shook their heads. "And Madam has height as well," the second one accused.

A young girl in black swayed her way down the aisle between the counters, bearing on her arm a sheaf of frocks and followed by a prospective customer. The cloth of her dress creased and recreased deliciously as she walked suggesting all kinds of agreeable stresses. Her hair was coiled in a bright helmet round her head and as she passed she raised green eyelids in surprise and said, "Oh – Miss Vincent!"

"Angela!"

"You know Angela?" the saleswoman asked, softening.

"I taught her."

"Did you? Did you hear that, Miss McLoughlin? Madam taught Angela – such a clever girl!"

"I'm glad you think so."

"And such a quick learner," said Miss McLoughlin,

131

giving Sarah unwelcome credit, "we are always glad when we get a girl like Angela."

Sarah's shares rose and the women turned again to the racks of dresses ranged in long glass cases with renewed determination. This customer had become a professional challenge and for Angela's sake she must be clothed. One after another they pulled gowns out, thrust them under Sarah's chin, consulted the label, and frowning pushed them back into the case again.

"Don't trouble – please."

Their desire to succeed was as disconcerting as their apathy had been.

"No trouble, none at all."

"But really – if you've nothing – it's hardly worth your while —"

Forget about it, forget about me, just let me creep out quietly when you aren't looking, let me make an orderly and decent retreat, that's all.

"The pink, Miss McLoughlin."

"Forty-six – no good."

"The moss-green?"

"Too short!"

"Perhaps the grey?"

They sped from case to case, whisking the dress-hangers along their rails in a strident frenzy.

At last a brown and white blotched garment, another in regal purple, and one in a shade which Miss Fennimore had worn – it had been known as Saxe Blue – were segregated as not wholly impossible.

"But I don't think – really —"

"You can't be sure until you try, can you, Madam?" they coaxed firmly.

As those who still have faith in miracles they conveyed Sarah to a dressing-room and smiled encouragingly at her as they drew the little curtains and shut her in. It was a flimsy prison but one from which there was no escape. She felt sick with panic, humiliation and most of all with annoyance at her own incompetence in this sort of a situation. The dresses from their hangers menaced her. Oh God, I must try them. I must undress and try them on.

She looked through a crack in the curtains. The women were chatting. Perhaps – but one of the women looked up sharply. Sarah drew the curtains a little closer and unbuttoned her coat.

It was Helen's fault. It was coming back to the house that did it after I had taken Helen to the airport. It was so quiet. The baby was asleep in his pram, Felicity stretched flat on the grass beside it. Gerald in his deck-chair with his hat tilted over his eyes was sleeping too; the cat was asleep on his lap. No one noticed me when I came in. No one greeted me. It was like the courtyard of the Sleeping Beauty's castle. Addie wasn't back from school yet. The hall door lay open. The house, emptied of Helen, already ached for her. The hall, when I entered it, was warm with undisturbed sunlight.

The second post had come and there were letters on the table, some of them for Helen. I picked them up, intending to leave them in her room. "Don't forward anything," she'd said, "it's just a nuisance for you, and anyhow I'll be here and there, and it's only for a week. Business letters will go to the shop."

I knew then that she wasn't going to tell me after all. I thought and had hoped that she would tell me just before she left. Sometimes she does things like that, as if she were measuring me with a kind of loving cruelty. But not today. When her flight was announced she said, "I expect I'll be in London mostly. But isn't it heavenly to cut loose, get right away from things – you know, Sarah." She took my hands, smiling, and put her face against mine for a moment while her perfume flowed round me, as if by this show of trust she was challenging me to ask her any questions. "Take care of yourself, Sarah my pet, and be good." I knew by the little exaggerations in her voice and the words she used that she had already, by whatever process she did it, surrounded herself with the faintly dramatic aura that she created when things were going well for her.

I took the letters up with me, and was going to leave hers in her room – I had her key – but I couldn't because when I reached the door I knew Papa was there. The room was Mama's bedroom and he was with her, so I couldn't go in and I left Helen's letters in the chest of drawers on the landing.

I have never known whether I admired or despised Papa for his loving care of Mama in the months before she died. I was called home in November but she didn't die until the summer. He was so kind to her, so gentle, so patient. He could have become again my Father on earth, co-partner of my Father in heaven, the way he used to be when I was a little girl, but since my illness I didn't need him any more. Miss Fennimore had been blotted out; she didn't exist either in his imagination or his memory – I could swear to that. Perhaps it didn't happen all at once, but she died a little every week all through that summer. Mama was frightened to die. I knew this although I would not let myself feel it. Papa both knew it and felt it for her. He sat hour after hour beside her bed, holding her hands in his, presiding over her. Sometimes he talked for long stretches at a time, sometimes they were silent. I felt that the words were not trivial or repentant or simply consolatory but that they had an active purpose both for him and her. I became more remote from my parents then than I had ever been, on the outside and yet not lonely. I neither needed nor wanted to intrude on them, and so when I heard his voice this afternoon I couldn't go in.

It was Wednesday and ordinarily the child Sally would have been here for her tuition but exams had started and she wasn't coming. If she had I might have comforted myself a little – only a little for the link was already broken. I have always tried to think of the love between my girls and myself as being something continuous, a perquisite of my office, a consequence perhaps of the noble lie, so that individual losses are unimportant to me. It is something passed from girl to girl as each outwears and outgrows it. It has been getting more and more difficult for me to do this.

I have often wondered what it must be like to be committed in mutual love. I am committed to Helen in my heart, but this is a private thing, an act performed singly that doesn't alter me in any way and imposes no responsibilities except those that I choose to assume. I cannot imagine that I would ever hesitate to assume them, but I must be free to choose. Part of the pleasure, perhaps, lies in the act of choice. But sometimes, as on this particular evening in the empty house I wondered what it must be like not to choose but to be chosen.

Those other sudden excursions that I make into friendship, the ridiculous ones that Helen laughs at, are just a sort of spending spree when I have some loose change in my pocket. I need to make them sometimes, like Addie did the other evening, with her ridiculous avowal. But to be committed to someone continually in mind and heart, so that you carry about with you a double image and every emotion is bilingual and every concern twofold would seem to confuse and impoverish experience beyond endurance. And to share my body is unthinkable.

I have never thought of my body since I was ill except as a point of location for my senses and my intelligence, a portable container. I have never expressed myself through it, as other women do. I have been glad that I am plain; it has been a protection and a liberation both. So what can I be doing now in this little tent of mirrors and curtains, standing in my petticoat confronted with these three impossible dresses, and those two dragons waiting for me outside.

I had gone upstairs to work, hoping to become involved in it. And then I looked at my watch and realised that Helen would be stepping off the plane by this time. I could see her, chin high, her lower lip full, and the corners of her mouth

135

drawn fractionally in. I wondered if Hubert was meeting her, or if she expected him. Perhaps she expected him and he would not come. I couldn't bear to think of that.

And then George rang. "Sarah?"

"Yes."

"Helen caught her plane?"

"Yes. She should be there by now."

"London, isn't it?"

I said yes, and waited for him to ask what else I knew but he didn't. Perhaps he didn't want to be told that I didn't know, perhaps he preferred me to think that she had told him. Anyhow he said, "I wondered if I could have a talk to you sometime, Sarah. You are one of the people I can talk to about Kitty."

"Kitty? Of course."

"Perhaps if we could meet —"

And keep tabs on each other, in case either of us has heard anything from Helen? It was tempting. All right, I'll play.

"What about tomorrow evening? Kitty will have a cousin visiting her tomorrow."

"I'd like that."

I was glad of a chance to talk about Kitty. It was a week since I had seen her, caught up as I was in the pace of end-of-term concerns. I could never reconcile George's solicitude for her with his insistence that her condition was beyond hope.

He suggested a restaurant and a time. And then I made my mistake. I suppose I did it because I was glad to hear from him and because it seemed a way out of my loneliness – that frantic summer evening loneliness with sunlight slanting into empty rooms – I said, "You come here, George. I'll give you a meal. It will be easier to talk."

I was crazy. I was completely lunatic. I didn't even at the time imagine myself offering any kind of a substitute for his evenings with Helen but I wanted to show some sort of kindness since I needed it so much myself. My room is a barracks, he knows that, and the kind of meal that I cook is something

on toast, mostly out of tins, and a pot of tea. I have no domestic graces or talents and no great flair for hospitality
except with my girls. But when he accepted and had hung up
I was filled with a wild enthusiasm to make a success of the
occasion, and today at lunchtime I went out and bought
haphazard quantities of food and some wine, and this was so
easy to do that when I saw the olive-green dress in the shop
window I charged in – and here I am, all three of me, reflected in the floor-length mirrors in this terrible dress, so that
I look like a three-piece suite in floral chintz.

When Helen buys clothes it is a serious affair because
clothes to her are an extension of her personality, in the way
that writing or conversation is to me, a kind of fulfilment.
Addie buys them as if by inspiration and impulse, imagining
that fate directs her, and by identifying herself with her
purchase she claims a right to its colour, gaiety, individu-
ality. I have a dressmaker to whom I take lengths of tweed
and who knows what to do with them – she has been doing
it for years, adding an occasional inch as required – and
when I find a cardigan that fits me I buy three of them at
the same time. I have a dark silk dress which I wear when
something more gracious is required, the third in a direct
line.

This floral horror was more difficult to get off than it had
been to put on. At last she was disengaged and stood dishevelled, her substantial thighs evident through the unsubstantial fabric of her slip, and as she bent forward to replace
it on the hanger she looked at the solid reflection of her arms
and bosom, her breasts pendulous from a deep dividing
valley, a subject for Rubens.

The curtains parted and the saleswoman's head appeared.

"Have you found what suits you, Madam?"

"No, no." She waved a hand at the flowered dress, dismissing it. Half-naked one must be doubly emphatic. "No
use. None at all."

"The purple, perhaps —"

137

The curtains closed again. Perhaps the purple. She reached for it resignedly. The fabric was soft and rich.

"Oh, Miss Vincent, could I help?"

Emerging from the neckline Sarah said, "Oh, Angela, I wish you would."

"It *is* nice to see you, Miss Vincent."

The girl was quick and deft. Sarah's flesh didn't rebel while she patted, coaxed, pulled, eased, with sympathy and respect.

"It is such a beautiful gown. A deep breath while I do the zip, Miss Vincent."

No breath was deep enough.

"It's no use," Angela said sadly, "it won't go on."

"I don't know what to do." Sarah's voice was getting wild. "I don't know what she will say. She just looks through me as if I weren't human." (Have I not hands, organs, dimensions, senses, affections, passions? But that would be lost on Angela.)

"You don't have to mind her," the girl soothed, "it's just her way. But it is a pity, the purple is nice, and good with your skin, Miss Vincent."

A kind girl, understanding, balanced.

"A firmer foundation might help," Angela suggested.

At this point Angela took command and in intimacy that Sarah could not have believed possible she was furnished with a foundation – another nymph assisting – and when the purple was replaced the zip closed sleekly. It looked remarkably well, investing Sarah with a kind of elegant nobility.

"There! What did I tell you?"

The pretty child was quite flushed with pleasure. Sarah studied her reflection. "I'm afraid my hair is terrible," she apologised. Angela, it seemed, had a friend in the Beauty Parlour on the top floor who would be flattered to be allowed to do Miss Vincent's hair. Such strong hair, so thick. "We always said at school that you had such thick hair, Miss Vincent."

138

After an hour and a half in the perfumed breezes of the Beauty Parlour Angela came to pass judgement. "Oh, it is good, Miss Vincent. Dignified. Just your style. It's lovely, Mavis." This is what a cat feels like, stepping off a satin cushion nourished with cream. Yes, Angela, I suppose we might need something from the Cosmetics Boutique. Yes, dear, you choose them for me, that would be splendid. Yes, that – and that – and that if you say so.

Angela went with her to collect her dress from the Gowns Salon, and as she entered the lift with the box under her arm Sarah looked back. Angela was standing between the two saleswomen, all three were smiling, nodding her good-bye. It occurred to her that Angela was, as they had said, a clever girl.

The room looked terrible. She spread her parcels out on the settee. It was later than she had realised, George was due in an hour. Panic mounted and she put on the new dress to reassure herself, trying to retain her uplifted mood as long as possible. She studied her reflection. The dress was all right. Something was missing. She made a little feminine gesture, shrugging and spreading her hands like the saleswoman had done. In some obscure way it seemed indecent. She tied an apron firmly round her unfamiliar purple waist and commenced to unwrap what she had bought.

The cooked chicken was still warm, the lettuce had flopped, she had forgotten the dressing, the cream for the fruit spurted as she whipped it. String and paper were everywhere, books pushed aside cascaded on to the floor. And she had not brought any flowers. The foundation nipped a little as it asserted itself, and her head was aching. She drank a quick glass of sherry and made a firm attempt to become mistress of the situation. She would slice the cucumber. She cut her thumb.

Flowers – I must have flowers – I can get some from the garden, there are plenty in the tangled bushes. A branchy arrangement of sprays would look well on the bookcase; not as good as Helen's, I know, but that sort of thing can't be so very difficult, everyone does it. But Addie and Gerald are walking down there, and I cannot appear in this astonishing garb without questions being asked, nor can I go stampeding through a shrubbery dressed like this. I could take it off, but would I be able to get it on again? We must do without flowers. Meanwhile I have lost the carving knife (there used to be a carving knife) the home-made dressing on the stove has boiled over and the room reeks of warm vinegar, there are splashes of cream on my new bosom and my thumb is still bleeding. I should like to laugh, but if I laugh now all is lost. And my hair is collapsing. Besides there is my face – which did the girl say I was to put on first? And wine glasses – wine glasses —

She pushed her hair back and took another sherry, moving with frantic muddled haste among parcels, plates and paper, achieving nothing.

At the end of half an hour she sat down defeated and rang up George. He was surprised.

"Sarah? Nice to hear you. But I'll be round in half an hour."

"No. It's no good, George. You can't come."

"What did you say?"

"I said – you can't come."

"You sound peculiar, Sarah. Is there anything the matter?"

"It's just that I can't have you. I'm sorry, George —"

"Of course if it's inconvenient, but —"

"Don't argue," she snapped.

"You aren't ill, are you?"

"I have a headache." Fool, fool, any other woman than you would have thought of that one straight away.

"A headache? Oh, bad luck. Well if you aren't feeling up to it —"

"I'm not. I'm sorry George. It's the end of term. We've been rushed to death."

"Of course. Well, let me see – Friday perhaps?"

"Friday's no use."

"Next week then. I could make it Tuesday."

"I'm not sure."

"In the afternoon. I'll call round for you. Good-bye, Sarah. I hope you'll soon be better."

He had hung up before she could reply. A rack of singeing toast that she had forgotten called her into the kitchen.

There was a knock at her door as she reached the toaster. She stood irresolute, thought of hiding in the pantry, turned, but the purple draperies caught on the door handle and held her captive. Maurice came in.

"Addie said she thought you were at home. So I came on up."

She blew out the last piece of toast, coughing at the smoke, disentangled herself and glowered at him from under the wreckage of her hair. Maurice, of all people.

"Hallo, Maurice. What do you want?"

He forgot at that moment what he had wanted although the necessity had been urgent. He had come in full flight from his ripely pregnant wife, from the fascination of the child's body whose shape he could now feel stirring in hers, from the threat of paternity, from Mary's continual visitations and the long intimate conversations she had with Florence about child-bearing, from their terrifying absorption in it, from the nursery already budding bunnies and bows, from this extension of himself that became every week more evident and more alarming. Sarah could give him refuge and restore his sense of proportion. He would go to Sarah.

Here she was, theatrical in purple, surrounded by a chaos of food. Her curious behaviour needed an explanation and excused him for the moment from offering one himself.

"Sarah! What is going on? Is this a fancy-dress party or something? You look like Lucretia Borgia cooking up one of her little messes. Or the Sibyl about to utter. You aren't the

141

Queen of Hearts, are you? I give up, you'll have to tell me. What are you doing, for God's sake?"

Surprisingly Sarah put the still-smoking rack of toast down on a pile of books and began to giggle an account of what had happened. She had intended to give a party. She had a headache and had decided to put it off. Now she was trying to clear up the mess.

"Quite a party," he said, moving the bottle of wine to a less precarious position. "It seems I have come just in time. A banquet for the Marquis of Carrabas!"

He said it because he was still out of his depth with her, and a little play-acting was the easiest way of marking time, but he was astonished when Sarah matched his mood, bowed deeply in that absurd garment, declaring, "Whatever your Luminous Magnificence wishes! Is it not always a most delicious honour when your Exquisite Person chooses to honour my slum-like abode with the summer sun of his all-glorious entirety?"

After that it went like a bomb. Restraint dissolved. He was filled with a huge affection for her. All the old gags, the old jokes. They remembered the rules as if it was only yesterday. He collected the chicken and other items of food haphazard on the low coffee table. "Untouched by human foot," he announced, and she laughed and placed cushions on the floor on to which they lowered themselves, sitting cross-legged. The folds of Sarah's elegance rippled round her. Maurice's waist-coat sat up uneasily over his stomach. The Napoleonic pallor of his face glowed with goodwill.

"Tell me, my dear Marquis, how many conquests have you made since last I basked in the glow of your twin-eyed regard? How many tall cities have toppled to your all-conquering spears?"

"Babylon and Ballybog, Kansas City and West Hartlepool," the Marquis of Carrabas announced as he poured the wine and joined her in drinking his health. They pulled joints from the chicken with their fingers and dipped them in salt and gnawed.

"And how many scented blossoms have you plucked for your harem since the last new moon mounted the sky?"

"Five hundred and seventeen – if you count the little one that squints," the Marquis said, refilling the glasses.

She should now have inquired how many noble sprigs had been born to him, but she missed that one out. It was surprising how hungry they were. They pulled the lettuce apart, bit into tomatoes, broke rolls and scooped them through butter.

"Now tell me what you're doing dolled up like that?" Maurice asked at last, wiping his fingers on his handkerchief and pushing it back into his pocket. "There's another glass apiece – pass yours over."

She told him about the shopping expedition and Angela, improving the story as she went. He roared with laughter.

"All the same – that dress!"

"'What word is this that hath escaped the portal of thy lips'? Don't you like it?" Sarah grieved. She heaved herself stiffly to her feet. "I'm not made for sitting this way any more. Neither are you, Maurice. You're putting it on a bit, aren't you? What does Joyce think of that?" She made indifferent coffee which they drank with islands of whipped cream afloat in it. Maurice shifted to a more comfortable seat on the sofa beside her.

"All these —" Sarah waved a hand at the battery of cosmetics. "Whatever will I do with them?"

Maurice selected the eyebrow pencil and made a neat moustache for himself. She drew tribal markings with the lipstick on her cheeks. Then he unscrewed the other little pots, sniffing and dabbing a blunt forefinger here and there. An odour of flowers spread through the room.

"Don't!" Sarah said unexpectedly, "you're messing them up!"

"But you don't want this sort of stuff! You! Whatever would you do with it?"

143

He should not have said that. It was a mistake.

"I expect I was very silly really," Sarah said stiffly. "I don't really know how it all happened."

Suddenly the party was on the ebb. "Oh, I don't know," he shrugged, trying to reclaim it, "that dress is really rather splendid in its way."

It was no use. Sarah had already begun to condemn herself and needed his support.

"Maurice, I was crazy. This is a ridiculous dress for me. Well, isn't it? You know I look ridiculous. Go on, take a look – look at me! Don't I look ridiculous? What on earth did I buy it for?"

Her voice had risen. How many glasses had she had? He couldn't remember. He just wished that things could have gone on for a little longer.

"I don't know why I do things like this," she mourned.

"Don't exaggerate. It isn't as if you went around making a habit of it."

"I know. But *why*. That's what I want to find out – why. She was leaning towards him, her large eyes mournful and solemn.

"Maurice why do I? A dress like this?"

She plucked at her bosom. She isn't drunk. She has just reached the earnest self-analytical stage. Any moment now she will become intimate and embarrassing and it will all be spoiled.

"Do you know what they call me at school, Maurice? Well – go on – guess! What do you think they call me?"

"Look, have some more coffee. Forget what I said. I like the dress. Honest I do."

"They call me Daddy Vincent! Well, what do you think of that? Daddy Vincent! Quite good, don't you think? Well, go on – don't you think it's quite good?"

"I was never much use at schoolgirl humour," he dodged. The inspiration of the party had trickled away and was being replaced by an unpleasant sincerity. Sarah had shocked and offended him. He took out his handkerchief again to wipe the moustache from his lip. It came, greasily. "You'd better clean yourself up, hadn't you?" he suggested. She ignored the suggestion.

"Daddy Vincent. I don't suppose you're surprised, are you? Well – are you?"

"Look, it's been a lovely party but I must go now, Sarah. Joyce is expecting me." He stood up, straightening his jacket, ridding himself of crumbs, tugging unhappily at his waistcoat.

"But you must agree it's appropriate, Maurice."

She stood up, dwarfing him, and squared herself like a man, posturing with her legs apart. "My feet – they're bigger than yours."

He took his neat plump shoe away from her large one.

"I must go."

"Don't you see, Maurice? And my hands." She spread them and enveloped his own.

"Joyce will be waiting." He disengaged himself.

"Oh – all right."

She came with him as far as the first flight, neither of them spoke. Then she said, "I won't come any further, Maurice. Addie's sure to be hovering."

Looking back at her he thought she appeared white, tired, dishevelled of course and a little lonely.

"Are you all right, Sarah?"

"Of course I am. Thank you for coming."

"Good night, then."

"Good night."

His voice was kind. She watched him as he went down the stairs and crossed the hall. What a pity it had ended like this. It had been pleasant, this party with Maurice. It was time now to go and bid good night to Mama before she fell asleep.

It was no use. She couldn't go in. Papa was there, he was still talking. His rich voice, accommodating itself to Mama's bedroom, went on and on interminably. She could not hear what he was saying. Even if she could have heard it she knew it was something she would not understand. Even its tone excluded her.

A panic of loneliness seized her. They must let her in! They must let her in!

Addie heard the hammering and came out of her flat. "Sarah," she called up the stairs. "Sarah! Is that you? What is it? Is anything the matter?"

Chilled suddenly to full reality Sarah called back "Nothing Addie. Sorry if I disturbed you. Helen's door was banging, that's all."

"Are you sure? Shall I come up? Sarah – are you all right?"

"I told you – it was Helen's door."

Sarah in purple trailed upstairs to bed.

CHAPTER ELEVEN

"I'M all right now, really I am," Addie declared, gratified by the faint flutter her collapse had made in the Staff Cloakroom at the end of afternoon school. "There was no need to fuss. I felt a little dizzy, that was all. Invigilating all day – it's the smell, I think, fruit gums and perspiration and tears and ink. But thank you for the lift."

She got out of Sarah's car and stood for a moment smiling doggedly and holding on to the door.

"You look pretty rotten. And you're crazy not to tell Gerald, you know."

"Gerald has other things on his mind just now, poor lamb. I know the signs. One of these evenings he will go out to post a non-existent letter and come home hours later descanting with the seraphim and blind to the world." Addie's face, still grey and pinched, savoured the prospect. "Sarah, don't you envy men? I'm glad Helen is away, all the same. She won't hear him. Helen is so critical." She paused, to see if Sarah was going to be drawn, and dared a little further. "She can be hard sometimes, don't you think? Anyhow, I know *you* understand."

Her eyes embraced Sarah, who took her by the elbow to help her across the gravel. She stumbled and laughed. "Must look where I'm going. My dear, did you see the bit on the tele about the bloodhounds? Fascinating, it was. That fold of skin falls down over their foreheads so that they can't see, because they smell their way much better if they don't use their eyes! Would you believe it? I dote on that man anyhow, don't you? Anything he tells me is intriguing."

"Come on," Sarah urged, "neither of us is a bloodhound."

The afternoon post would have arrived, there might be a

letter from Helen. Since lunch time she had been edgy with anticipation. So far there had been nothing, no news. This meant that things were going well for her. How well? Or badly, perhaps. How badly? In any case, which did she hope for?

There were two letters for Addie, one of them the weekly Airmail, but none of any kind for Sarah. Addie went into her flat, promising to lie down for half an hour and go early to bed. "How kind you are, Sarah! Doesn't it seem quiet without Helen in the house?"

Sarah went upstairs. She had work to do. But she was tired and sat at the window with her books in front of her, staring out, drained, confused, aching for news of Helen, irritated by Addie's endless cadging for firmer friendship, still annoyed when she remembered the antics she had been involved in with Maurice, thinking uneasily of Kitty to whom she owed more than one visit.

Florence rang, asking for a cake for a Cake Fair. "Florence, don't be absurd, you know I can't bake." "It is for the Children." "Talking of children, your grandson's thriving; he lies in my garden getting fatter and fatter." Florence changed her public voice to her private one and said "I don't see very much of them, you know." "I'll send you a cheque, shall I?" "Would you? That would be sweet of you." Sarah wrote a cheque, feeling guilty that fifty of the world's children could so easily be furnished with a daily glass of milk for a month.

Mr. Boyd's nephew had not cut the long line of daffodils that edged the lawn. It was time they were cut, more than time, for the leaves had withered weeks ago into a dense fringe of grass, buttercups and dandelions. The wood-pigeon was there, making a leisurely raid on the tall seeded grasses. He ambled along on thick pink feet, pausing to strip a stem in a succession of accurate staccato pecks. The mauves and blues and greys of his plumage – bubble colours – shifted with every stab. The white collar which did not quite meet round his neck might have been made by the finger and thumb of a painter who had held him while his brush applied the colours.

She envied the bird its self-sufficiency and decision. Life, in so far as it presented her with any further development, seemed to offer two choices – to remain detached and emphatic like this bird, ignoring self-distrust (and eventually, unlike the bird, to qualify as an eccentric) or in the draughty corridor of middle-age to expose herself to every wind of opinion and influence that blew and end up in the doldrums of mindless indecision. She would have been willing to settle for the first course, but now she felt that the pressure of personal relationships was tugging her in the other direction.

She flipped through her desk-diary, trying to restore some sense of purpose in herself, and discovered with consternation that this was Tuesday. Tuesday. Her life was geared to a school time-table and when this was upset for examinations she was lost. Lost indeed, since this was Tuesday.

She pushed her books aside, there was no time to waste. She seized her porridge-coloured coat and tam. Escape was essential. Anywhere. Anywhere. The telephone bell called to her as she reached the top of the stairs, but it only put spurs to her flight.

She was already too late. George turned in at the gate just as she reached the front steps. He was walking briskly, wearing a crisp orange rosebud in his buttonhole. The sun which had darkened his face shone on his thick white hair so that he looked like a demigod out for a stroll among mortals. Momentarily she was terrified. The man for whom I was ready to make a fool of myself, for whom I dolled myself up, bought perfumes, made an effort for the first time in my life.

She engaged all her critical faculties at once and succeeded in seeing him not as a demigod but as a tailor's dummy, ageless, well-nourished, pleased with himself. This didn't help her, because if he was pleased it meant that Helen had written to him. She became sure of it. Helen had telephoned, they had talked and laughed together in a language she didn't understand. And before she hung up Helen perhaps had sent her a message and George was bringing it. So he wins.

"I can't see you, George," she said wildly, "I know you said Tuesday and I meant to phone but we've been so busy at school that I forgot."

He raised experienced eyebrows. "Surely – for a moment —"

I don't want to be told what Helen said, to be handed affection second-hand, or to be told by you that she has been to see Hubert and speculate with you on what this could mean.

"No. No. I told you. I'm sorry. I have to go out."

There must be some foolproof and acceptable female errand. I have an appointment at the hair-dresser's, I have a fitting with the dressmaker. What did other women say?

"Can I leave you anywhere," George suggested. "My car's on the road."

"No, you can't. I am —" a lion roared high up on the hillside and she thanked it silently and said "I am taking a party of my girls to the Zoo."

George didn't answer. Silence gaped. She felt him staring. He looked at the empty gravel and said gravely, "Are they all here?"

"George —"

"I am sure they wouldn't object if I came along as well," he said. "Forward! The Zoo! You and I will head the procession."

Absurdity led her by the nose, there was no escape. She and George were going to the Zoo. They walked, it was not a long distance. The afternoon was hot. On their right the lively Lough water leapt. They passed from deep shadow to strong sunlight under arching trees. Suburban pavements were blowsy with tufted grass sprouting along the cracks. She inquired for Kitty. He gave the formal replies. She waited for news of Helen. He didn't offer any. So he was biding his time, was he?

"Two adults," he said, putting his four shillings down as they went through the turnstile. The woman in the kiosk recognised George's face and simpered, and then peered curiously at Sarah whom she obviously thought was an unlikely companion. "I could be your aunt or your cousin up from the country," Sarah suggested, and was glad when he looked annoyed. She had by this time recovered her courage and some of her balance. The situation was amusing. Very well, I will fight you for Helen. Fight you tooth and claw. A Zoo is an appropriate place. I have loved her longer and better than you have. And I know her more intimately, not her body, but her mind. Before you can give me any news of Helen I will tell you how well I understand her, establishing my precedence over you. I will go over her with a reminiscent microscope for your benefit, expounding on her virtues, faults, habits, impulses, fears, enthusiasms, dislikes – her childhood and girlhood, reducing her stature by an analysis of its parts, so that anything you have to tell me about her is something that my own knowledge will have made a foregone conclusion.

The Demoiselle Crane picked her path fastidiously through rank grasses. "Pretty things," George said, "so completely feminine."

She talked about Helen in the nursery, completely feminine, Helen in bows and laces at Christmas parties, the dancing class they attended together, Helen always in the chief role at displays, of her successes as Fairy Queen, Ice Maiden, Sleeping Beauty.

"What were you?" George asked.

"Me? Something in the back row. But Helen —"

They walked through the reptile house where behind heavy plate glass the snakes had tidied themselves into motionless and improbable coils, and found beyond it a solitary penguin sulking on bald concrete in front of a tepid pool.

"Poor fellow," George said, "all on his own. Hasn't he any pals?"

She talked about Helen at school, always at the hub of a circle of friends. "Everyone liked her, she had a gift for it, I suppose. Even then she was the kind of person who needed to be liked – you know what I mean. And beautiful, always beautiful, even in a gym tunic and black stockings."

She told him about the Art Master with the tubercular wife and all those children and how he made surreptitious sketches of Helen, and how they were discovered and he had left at the end of the term. "Hair down to her waist – everyone else was getting it bobbed or shingled, it was the rage just over from the States, but Helen kept her hair long."

The monkeys were indoors today. The hall smelt of sawdust and orange peel and monkey flesh, and vibrated with yelps, cackles, screams, and sudden attacks upon the thick wire mesh.

She talked about Helen growing up, of her strings of admirers, of the fun she had with them – "she used to tell me about it."

"Did you tell her about your affairs?"

"There weren't any," she said, and knew he was outraged, not by the fact but by her admission of it. She went on talking about Helen. A little ginger capuchin monkey dredged unsuccessfully through the wire for a peanut just beyond his reach. George leaned over the barrier and pushed the nut into the small black hand with the point of his umbrella.

Half-way through the monkey house she remembered its potential embarrassments and was annoyed with herself for pressing on to the safety of the last cage where a mother embraced a passive baby. The infant was a miniature of the parent with none of the endearing softness of childhood. It reminded Sarah of the Christ manikin in early pictures. Across its head the mother stared at them, defying their criticism.

George said, "I suppose she loves it, heaven knows why. Did your parents love you, Sarah?"

"I don't know. I never allowed my mother to be anything more than an emblem. They wanted me to love them, I think."

They climbed the long brutal concrete steps that led to the highest tier of cages. Sarah grew breathless, her leg ached. She was glad to notice that George's pace slowed a little. A couple of young things in slacks with hair bouncing on their shoulders and taut bottoms see-sawing leapt past, overtaking them. "These steps are hardly intended for our age-group, George," she smiled. His personal beast, who was squatting on his shoulder beside his buttonhole made a face at her. They reached the top and a reindeer loped across its paddock to examine them and finding them uninteresting returned to crop grass.

Two girls on a seat sucking ice lollies noticed George and identified him. They nudged and giggled.

"Two of your fans," Sarah said, "you are observed. Is it true that they write letters to you?"

"Some of them do."

"What do they say?"

"That they love me very much and would like to marry me. They are sure they could make me happy. Will I please stroke my cheek with my left hand when I say good night on Tuesday because that is their birthday and they will know it is specially meant for them. Some of them hate my guts."

Inside his bars the tiger reclined on the crest of the rise, startling and immaculate. He was enjoying the fine day and the view of Belfast Lough spread out below him, trees, hills and water whose surface was criss-crossed by dark unaccountable liquid ribbons, a checkboard of fields on the hills rising from the further shore, spires, chimneys, roof-tops, a housing estate sedate as children's bricks, a mill dam throwing back the sky's colour, the cemetery to the left with memorial stones

153

white like bones, and far up the Lough the angles and heights of the shipyards.

There was a crowd round the cage, admiring, exclaiming, taking photographs, holding up their children. The animal stared steadfastly over their heads, superbly indifferent, and pulled a casual growl out of nowhere with barely a movement of his throat.

"He has a beautiful view," she said.

"A limited one."

"So long as he realises that," and she led the way to the Chimpanzee.

They found him striding his few yards of territory waving a piece of sacking. Sometimes he made a flag out of it, sometimes a carpet, a hood, a swaddled infant. Eventually he wrapped it round his shoulders like a cloak, wasn't satisfied with the result, tried again, and came over to the bars and peered out to see how Sarah dealt with the problem of clothing. He appeared unimpressed.

"Tea – come on," George said, "I saw a café somewhere, something with chips and sauce-bottles."

All through the fried eggs she talked to him about Helen and Hubert. "Right from the beginning there didn't seem to be any question about it. They were meant for each other. You only had to see them together to know." Clichés clicked from her masticating teeth, she despised herself and went on talking. "He was very tall, very blond, very English. Glorious Apollo, we called him. It was frightening how much they were in love. We were bridesmaids. I will never forget their faces when they took the vows. They never looked at anyone but each other."

Tell me now that you have heard from her and that she is going back to him. I am ready. How can it surprise or distress me? He said nothing. She refilled his cup.

"You never met him, of course, did you? And then there was the little girl."

She was struck suddenly dumb and could say no more. She

154

felt her face flame with shame and the hot food. "I'm a fool," she said, "a fool."

The waitress set thick glass goblets in front of them, containing tough elastic jelly that tasted like communion wine. George began to talk about Kitty. "The first thing I noticed about her was how shy she was. She was always shy. I was never used to shyness. It isn't my strong point. It was terribly attractive. I thought it would give us a kind of ultimate sincerity that I couldn't arrive at with one of my own kind. God, Sarah, how tough a shy woman can be. An armour, not a shell. I am always naked with her, in bed or out of it. She never is. Sometimes when she is tired she allows herself to be my child. You can't offend against a child. She knows that."

Sarah pressed small spoonsful of jelly against her palate, retaining it as long as she could. He had never talked this way before. There was no way of stopping him.

"You can't play doll's house for ever," he said.

The waitress brought his bill and Sarah collected her gloves. When they left the café the cool air helped her. Light had drained from the sky, only the western horizon was barred and slotted with orange whose colour was reflected in small scattered shawls of cloud drifting over the faded heaven. The lights in the amusement park were lit, necklaces of red, blue and green, stringing the trees. The colour of grass and leaves had deepened to a green that burned. There was laughter, and somewhere a cheap love-syrupy tune.

The children had gone home, there was no more shouting and racing, no more slapping, scolding or the run of pram wheels. Couples trod the paths with the ceremonial pace of lovers, leaving a drift of perfume or cigarette smoke as they passed. It was a foreign country to Sarah and she realised that all she had shown George of Helen had no more significance than an album of faded photographs, compared with his own knowledge of her. I know all the little things. She had long hair, she was pretty at school, she was bad at French, moths used to frighten her, she needed to have friends, she

155

was fond of pink, she was radiant on her wedding day. He knows her in that terror of intimacy of which I have no experience, he has shared her skin, her breath, her warmth, her waking, the needs of her body as it grows older, her humility.

George slid his hand under her elbow as they came down the path, and his arm touched the side of her breast. It happened to her in that single moment, throat, stomach, thighs, a whole new dimension of feeling. She fought to stop herself from trembling, and prayed he would not know. They reached the road, and he talked of Kitty again, as if he were preparing himself to go home to her.

"And you'll call in with her on Wednesday, Sarah? She always looks forward to your days."

They had reached the gate of Thronehill and halted. "You expect absolution," she said angrily, "I'm not qualified, you know."

"Would you give it if you could?"

"No. And I won't ask you in, George. I have work to do "

She was turning when he caught her elbow; his nearness terrified her She clenched her hands to prevent herself from embracing him.

"A minute, Sarah. I meant to ask you. Have you had any word from Helen?"

"No. Nothing. Nothing at all."

He said, "I just wondered. Neither have I. Not a word."

She had left him and was half-way up the avenue when she began to laugh, not with amusement but out of joy for an experience which she had so nearly missed. If at her age her plain and defended body could receive it, what must it be like in youth? She left the path and went into the shrubbery, appalled and delighted, laughing when branches of laurels tangled in her hair.

She reached the summer-house, still laughing, and halted on the threshold in case Papa was there. He often sat there during the time when Mama was dying. Though she had rallied on Sarah's return from England she grew weaker as spring came and lengthened into summer. Now his talking exhausted her. Perhaps it had achieved its purpose. "The illness is taking its normal course," the doctor said. The weeks dragged. The whole house now was occupied with her dying. Papa couldn't bear to sit indoors any more except when he was in Mama's room. "I'll be in the summer-house, you can call me." He sat there in the dusk with his unread newspaper, watching the light of the sickroom window shining on the lawn.

Sarah was in her room, exhausted with tension and miserably impatient for her mother's death when the nurse called from the corridor, "Your father, Miss Vincent, tell him to come at once." And she ran downstairs and crossed the grass to the summer-house.

"You are to go to Mama. You are to go at once."

He sat hunched and didn't move. They had all been waiting for this and yet she knew he didn't want to go. He was afraid he would fail her. For thirty years of unrelenting habitual affection his voice had been the first she had heard every morning, the last every night. Once more, one last, tremendous time.

The bedroom window opened.

"Mr. Vincent – hurry!"

The nurse's voice was sharp and unprofessionally urgent. Papa rose slowly and crossed the lawn.

But tonight the summer-house was empty, a three-sided box of shadow and spiders, and there was no light from Mama's room.

Sarah straightened her clothes and her hair and went on to the house.

Addie came out from her door as she entered the hall. Her hair was tightly netted, she was cocooned in a dressing-gown.

"There you are Sarah – come in for a minute."

"Addie – is something the matter? Is it Gerald?"

"Gerald is in bed and asleep. Where have you been?"

157

"Walking – walking," she said, "and why didn't you go off early like you promised?"

In Addie's sitting-room the television set was on. Two girls in diaphanous draperies sat on a moonlit cloud and enlarged to sugar-plum music on the merits of a certain deodorant.

"I mistrust a generation that is deluded like that, don't you?" Addie said, "it seems more honest to smell." She turned it off.

"Why aren't you in bed, Addie?"

Addie looked self-important and said "There was a wire for you. They tried to get you on the phone, then they rang me. I wrote it down."

The slip of paper said 'Flying back tomorrow. Look forward so much to seeing you. All love. Helen.'

"Helen's coming back tomorrow," Sarah said unnecessarily.

Addie said brightly, "That's nice, isn't it? You'll be so much happier now."

CHAPTER TWELVE

"AND everything is exactly the same!" Helen declared joy-fully, looking at her reflection in the mirror of the Hotel bed-room – the one they had every summer – and including her own face in the catalogue of things that were unchanged. "How marvellous it is to come back and find everything the same!" She turned and looked out of the window. "Except the sweet-pea – they're better than ever this year, Mrs. Dunne, I don't know how Mr. Dunne does it. Look at them, Sarah!"

"The wallpaper's new," Mrs. Dunne beamed. She had left her post at the reception desk and come with the chamber-maid and the hall-porter to convey the ladies upstairs. Their arrival had created an agreeable flutter. James the waiter and Kathleen the waitress came from the kitchen regions to greet them. James was large and majestic with a slight stoop that he had acquired through the pride he took in his professional humility. His face, long and solemn like a horse, struggled between pleasure at seeing them and his sense of what was fitting towards Hotel guests. Kathleen's hair was brassier than ever, her complexion powdered thickly over the red threads that netted her white skin. There was also a new boy in a white coat, bland and faceless like a seal, and smiling. Obviously he already knew these ladies by reputation.

"Such a business we had getting a paper to suit," Mrs. Dunne said, "seeing it was your room and knowing Mrs. Harris has such an eye for quality – Miss Vincent too, of course."

"It's beautiful, really beautiful! Isn't it, Sarah?"

Sarah muttered her admiration. She admired Helen's per-formance even more though it alarmed her. Helen had come back from London in so gay and animated a mood that it was nearly a caricature of herself, talked about everything except what she had done there, and had launched straight away into preparations to make a festival of their fortnight at the sea. "Of course I booked – ages ago. I must have told you."

It suited Sarah to indulge her. If Helen wanted to play dolls, all right she would play dolls. The game might help them both. On the evening before they left town she visited Kitty and was glad to find her alone. Kitty was withdrawn, almost hostile. It would have been easier if she had been difficult or disagreeable. Always with Kitty some other mood would have been easier. She wound her fingers through the ribbons of her bedjacket and looked at Sarah with a kind of remote amusement.

George came into the hall as Sarah was leaving. He said, "I wish you weren't going, she'll miss you." In this domestic setting Sarah was glad to see him as a tired and worried man, nothing else; so relieved indeed that she said warmly, "I wish things were better, George," but he avoided this. "How's Helen? I haven't seen much of her since she came back. She seems very gay." "Oh, she is, she is."

Back at Thronehill she found Helen with her room littered and the suitcases still unfilled. "I can't decide what to take – help me, Sarah!" She bullied Sarah into making decisions and then revoked them if it suited her and told Sarah what to pack. This was part of the ritual, the introductory movement to their closer association during the fortnight. Sarah, bruised by her failure with Kitty, succumbed to it and knew that Helen was pleased.

"My head aches. Nobody brushes my hair like you do, Sarah. Brush it for me."

The rhythmic movement of the brush and the feeling of Helen's hair in her hands, fragrant and silky, roused an ecstasy of tenderness in her. Helen sat with her head back, eyes closed, almost a girl's profile. "Lovely, lovely."

Felicity knocked and came in. "I'm sorry." She stood

hesitantly in the doorway as if she had intruded on an intimate scene.

Sarah put the brush down, feeling foolish. Helen said, "Come in, child."

Felicity looked untidy and exhausted. Her eyes were shadowed. She was wearing no make-up and a stained dressing-gown with draggled frills.

"It's about the laundry, Mrs. Harris; you said you wanted me to send your parcel off when he called."

"The laundry – how clever of you to remember. Just imagine – I'd forgotten all about it." She smiled at the girl and shrugged, playing for sympathy – a mind like a sieve, be sorry for me – but the girl's heavy face was unresponsive.

"Isn't it lovely to be going off on holiday?" Helen demanded, "we're so excited."

Felicity pushed her hair back. "I expect it is."

"We've done this every year for ages, Sarah and I. To the same place, but it's always wonderful. When do you and Justin go?"

"I don't expect we do. I don't think we can afford it, and there's the baby."

Helen smiled. "Next year then; it's something to look forward to."

"Unless there's another baby by then."

"My dear —" Helen hesitated, unsure of her ground. Her face, framed in the long hair that lay over her shoulders, looked a little grotesque like something out of pantomime.

"It must be very nice for you I'm sure," the girl said, unnecessarily loudly, "I hope you have a lovely time." She picked up the pile of laundry and went away.

They waited until the door had closed. Helen lifted the brush. "I'll finish it myself. No, don't fuss, Sarah, I said I'd finish it. She's an odd child, I don't think she meant to be rude. They let themselves go, these young things, when they have a baby. What she'll do with two – surely they can plan nowadays. Pills are so much more civilised."

Mrs. Dunne and her retinue left them and as the door closed the curtains at the open window lifted and swung, admitting the healthy salt breath of the sea. Helen kicked off her shoes and stretched back on her bed. "The wallpaper is hideous, isn't it? But wasn't it sweet of them to take so much trouble?"

They walked into the village before dinner and bought postcards and an evening paper in the usual little shop where they were welcomed like friends. Helen was on the top of her form; she had a gift for reclaiming acquaintance on a year-old thread. She went into the chemist's for a film. "I have your number waiting for you," the man said, "knowing you'd be here." The sailor with paralysed legs sitting on the chair at his cottage door greeted them. All down the steep street it was the same. Childishly Helen declared that dogs and cats remembered her, challenging Sarah to doubt it. "And the same seagulls!" she cried.

They owned the place before they went on to the pier to see the lighthouse swing its first beam, as they always did on their first evening of the holiday. They stood under the massive wall listening to the suck of waves against it. Light had nearly gone. The sky was packed with clouds crowded together like driven sheep. A yacht bucked and creaked at its moorings.

Helen stretched her arms wide, laying her palms against the lighthouse wall, embracing it. She put her cheek against it. "You can still feel the sun." Then she looked up at the lantern. "It won't be long now."

I do not know how I can condone these theatricals and still love her. Loving Helen is the only deliberate dishonesty I allow myself, and I justify it because I admit I am being dishonest. We are not two absurd middle-aged ladies playing dolls. We are women performing a rite. We have come back to the primal things, sun, sand, sky and sea. Our faces in the bedroom mirror are a year older, but these things do not change. After a year that has offered us nothing but small things we have come back for comfort and assurance from ribbed sand, the pattern of breaking water as it runs over a rock, clouds assembling before the wind; things that have been the same since we were children and will be the same long after we are dead. And though our bodies leave no children who will enjoy these things after us these elements have still the power to move us. But they move us in different ways. Helen identifies them with herself and wears them as ornaments. I have become separated from the nondescript woman who stands here and is grateful she is not beautiful, and I am the seagull, the wave, the cloud. Where the bee sucks there suck I, and twelve stone of me waits in my unimaginative shoes until I am ready to occupy them again.

The light above their heads shone out strongly, startling them although they had been expecting it, and wheeled and swung. They remembered the rhythm of it at once. It lit the row of houses edging the harbour in unfamiliar detail, the Church spire, the derelict castle, then it flashed out to sea, where the mist at once defined and limited its beam to a geometric form. Inland again, probing the sweet slope of the hill that rose behind the houses, curved like a woman's breast. Not my breast, Sarah thought, never mine.

"Home," Helen said. They turned back in the direction of the Hotel. She tucked her arm into Sarah's. "We must make our plans, we don't want to waste any of our fortnight, do we? What day did I tell you George was coming? I wonder who is at the Hotel this year."

It would matter very much to Helen who was at the Hotel. Hotel life presents a tempting stage for a dramatised version of one's domestic behaviour. Helen always gave a poised performance. Every year there had been someone to play opposite her. A Bank Manager, recently widowed. Helen had discussed her investments with him. A callow invalid lad who painted impossible Irish landscapes for tourist consumption. Helen became his critic. Last year there had been a vulgarly endearing commercial traveller. There must be someone.

Afterwards she laughed at them, but it was an appetite and must be fed.

"Come on, Sarah. How slow you are. James will wonder where we've got to."

Sarah discarded her coat in the hall, Helen went upstairs to repair her face and hair, making a business of checking that there were no letters for her in the letter-rack. "Such a relief to get away from it all!" They made their entrance, steering towards the table in the second bay.

James intercepted them. "Over here, Mrs. Harris."

His face was concerned, and in his large eyes a look that could have been apology or compassion.

Helen stopped in mid-flight. "But surely —"

Four people dining at the table in the second bay window looked up inquiringly.

James said, "We thought Miss Vincent and yourself might prefer this table. It's more of a size for two, maybe."

He indicated a small table against the wall. Helen didn't move.

"Will this suit you, Mrs. Harris?" his voice entreated.

The quartette in the bay window watched her over the rims of their suspended soup spoons.

"Why of course, James! This is a dear little table."

They sat down. Helen's face was flushed, there was a look of pride in James's eyes. Sarah felt weak with love and indignation.

Sarah growled, "This table is quite all right."

"That's what I said. But wasn't it sweet of James – he seemed quite worried in case we might be offended. He's got a little older, don't you think? Oh my God, Sarah – the flowers!"

She smiled at James when he offered her the menu and ordered her meal blithely.

"Who's the new lad, James?"

"His name is Stephen, Madam."

"Just a learner, is he?"

164

"He will be taking over from me next season."

"From you? But James —"

James bent his head. "It comes to us all, Madam."

"And will you be taking Kathleen with you when you retire?"

"That will be for her to say, Madam." James was a servant even in his love life.

They set about a little grimly enjoying their fortnight. They revisited old landmarks and exclaimed at finding them exactly where they had left them. They took picnic lunches and ate them where they had sprinkled last year's crumbs. They went to Church on Sunday, a small rectangular building full of peace and dust and sunlight, where the sound of waves competed with the preacher's voice. Inside the congregation was scanty, fisherfolk, shopkeepers, farmers and their families. Outside the gravestones of five generations of their forefathers thronged and jostled to the Church door. Sarah, whose courage had begun to ebb, prayed earnestly for the success of the holiday and wondered what Helen was praying for. She felt grateful that at least before the Throne of Grace one did not feel oneself an anachronism.

They wrote postcards to Addie, Florence, Mary, Joyce, Enid, Kitty. Helen made friends with the family who occupied the table in the second bay window. Sarah found her drinking sherry with them before dinner. "Come and be introduced, Sarah. Isn't it a relief, they haven't noticed the dreadful draught at that table – it used to slay us!" Helen decided the guests were a dull lot. "Let's hope there'll be somebody more interesting next week." The place was noisy with transistor sets.

On Tuesday George telephoned. "Mr. Pedlow is on the telephone, Madam," James told her. George's visit every year had a prestige value that the Hotel appreciated. This year in particular Helen would enjoy walking into the dining-room in front of him. But George, it seemed, couldn't come Friday, as he had hoped. He would try to come on

Sunday evening. "Mr. Pedlow will be here on Sunday, James."

"We will look forward to that, Madam."

Wednesday was wet and they went to the Pictures. It was a modern film, violent and raw. They were moved by it but uncomfortable at seeing it in each other's company. They would have preferred something nostalgic, George Arliss in *Disraeli*, or *Intermezzo* with Ingrid Bergman flapping around girlishly in her slacks.

Thursday again was wet, fine seaside rain that filled the air but did not seem to fall. They walked over the links, the bracken in the rough was weighted with soaked cobwebs. Sarah's leg was hurting, and her stomach had begun to rebel against Hotel food. No, there had been no telephone message in their absence. Helen was suddenly concerned about the flowers which her shop was supplying for a wedding on Saturday; she held long animated telephone conversations with her chief assistant. She told James about it during dinner. "If you want to be sure a thing is done properly, James, you must do it yourself." "Indeed yes, Mrs. Harris." Their coffee that evening was tepid. Helen said, "James is getting a little slow, don't you think?"

On Friday it was James's day off and Stephen looked after them. His service was quick and a little showy. There was a good deal of smiling between him and Kathleen. He forgot the caper sauce.

"I will go to see Miss Fennimore on Sunday," Sarah decided.

"You must be back before George goes. He'd be sorry if he missed you."

They sat on the sea front on Saturday afternoon. It was crowded with holiday-makers down from Belfast for the day. The children were beautiful, innocent, absorbed, amusingly naked. They did not find the nakedness of the young girls and men amusing. Sarah identified the navels of three of her sixth-formers, and one from the Upper Fourth. Helen

166

spent the evening in the bar with the family from the table in the second bay window. Sarah went to bed early with a sick headache and pretended to be asleep when Helen came up.

Sunday morning was cold, grey, raining, and a light perpetual wind that blew in all directions at once. They did not go out. On Sunday afternoon Helen surprisingly said that she would come with Sarah to visit Miss Fennimore. "George might be here." "Hardly before dinner time. If he is he can wait."

They walked across the shore which was deserted except for gulls. The rain was over and from the dividing clouds flat yellow sunlight fell sadly and without heat, as it does sometimes at the end of August. The tide had fallen, leaving pools.

The elderly ladies were housed in an elderly residence where high ceilings and rooms the size of tennis courts allowed the air to move restlessly above their stooped shoulders. For the most part they walked or sat singly in careful isolation from each other. Miss Fennimore was in a chair at the end of the sun parlour. Each year it took a moment to identify this old lady with Miss Fennimore although she had been pointed out. It was more difficult today since she was sitting with a rug round her knees and her eyes closed. The eyelashes, as plentiful as ever, were white now, instead of gold. Her hair was white but scanty. It had been cropped and the pink scalp was evident beneath it. Her hands, distorted with rheumatism, were the hands of age, veined and shiny, with brown patches on the back. They held an orange. Her chest, under the heavy knitted cardigan which was fastened closely under her chin with a brooch, rose and fell fractionally, as if her body now required a very small intake of air. Her chin and ears had become unnaturally elongated and had the fragile gleam of egg-shell.

"I think she's asleep," Helen said. "Oh dear, I wish I hadn't come."

The old lady opened her eyes at once and became Miss Fennimore, the 'Snowy Breasted Pearl' to whom Papa had sung when she played his accompaniments in the drawing-room at home.

"Well, this is nice!" she said.

Her colleagues on the adjacent chairs ignored the visitors completely, defending themselves from becoming members of a community.

"I won't get up, dear – do find somewhere to sit."

They pulled up chairs and ranged themselves like schoolgirls opposite her.

She scrutinised Helen. "Now who is this? No, don't tell me. Ah yes, I remember you. You are Helen. You used to come to tea. You always had style. That was what I used to say to myself 'That girl has style'. Not like our poor Sarah. Ah, you either have it or you haven't, that's right, isn't it? I was always grateful to be one of the lucky ones."

She smiled, using her eyelids the way she used to.

"How are you, Miss Fennimore?" Helen leaned forward, self-consciously solicitous and speaking a little too loudly.

"Well enough, thank you. I have to be, you know. We all have to be. Oh dear, yes." She laughed and dropped the orange. Sarah retrieved it and put it back into her fingers, remembering them years ago, small and defenceless, holding her hymnbook. "They give us an orange after lunch on Sunday. Well, that's kind, isn't it? The food is bad but you can't spoil an orange, can you? Your Mother always kept a very good table, Sarah. She was a wonderful woman. It was too rich for some complexions, perhaps, but I never had to worry." She patted her cheek.

They talked for half an hour. Miss Fennimore contributed most of it. She told them the small scandals of the place; it was surprising how much these individuals knew about each other. "And I expect you're still scribbling," she said to Sarah, "you always were a curious girl. I suppose it was all very well, but you missed so much. So much of life." She said to Helen, "You mustn't allow Sarah to let herself go, will you?"

At last they rose to take their leave. Miss Fennimore dropped the orange again and Helen brought it back. Her twisted fingers turned it over. "I hope it isn't bruised."

She kissed Helen. "So kind of you to come; so nice to see someone with style in this place!" Then she turned to Sarah catching her hands with unexpected strength. Her eyes searched Sarah's face and Sarah felt her breath, faintly musky. "No trace of your dear Papa," she said with infinite sadness. "No, not a trace."

The tide was coming in again, widening the pools and runnels. They picked their way through them across the sand. The captive water reflected light from the evening sky. Helen stooped to splash salt water against her cheek. "Oh my God, I wish I hadn't gone. Why didn't you tell me she was like that?" She dried her face with her handkerchief and said with brisk pity, "Poor old soul! Fancy dying when you've lived such a little life."

Sarah, hands plunged in her pockets, didn't look at her. "My father was her lover. In his own house. For years, while my mother was ill."

The wind caught at their voices. Helen jumped the next pool. "He amused himself, did he? Come on, Sarah, how slow you are."

Sarah floundered after her. "They were very deeply in love. It was like a torch."

Helen turned her head. "What did you say?"

"A torch."

They reached the Hotel in silence. There was no sign of George. Sarah put a comb through her hair and took a book into the Lounge. Helen went upstairs after she had made sure they had been allotted a table for three in the dining-room. She had already asked for it the previous night and reminded James this morning at breakfast.

At half-past seven Helen came downstairs. Sarah, hunched

over her book and seeing none of it, praying only for George to come, looked up. "There's no sign of him yet."

Helen was wearing a young girl's dress which made her upper arms thin and ugly and her hips angular. Her make-up was lavish. No young girl would have put on all that jewellery.

"You've laid it on a bit, haven't you?" Sarah said wretchedly. Helen ordered drinks. Stephen who brought them raised his eyebrows sufficiently to betray a silent wolf-whistle. "There was no need to dress up", Sarah barked; Helen's thick green eyelids flickered.

Eight o'clock and George had not yet arrived. Sarah was exhausted with expectancy. Other guests went through the Lounge. "Aren't you coming in?" "We're waiting for a friend." It was half-past eight before Helen rose and made a frozen and magnificent entrance into the dining-room. Sarah following caught the significant glances from the other tables.

"Mr. Pedlow has been unable to come, James."

"I am sorry to hear that, Madam."

Throughout the meal James served her with a passion of formality and love. Afterwards she went into the Bar and Sarah took her book upstairs to search for aspirin.

At eleven Helen came into the bedroom giggling. "My dear, we had such a good evening, why didn't you come? You always hide yourself away, it isn't social. Those people at our table, so amusing – do you know what they call James? 'The Horse Tram'. Isn't it gorgeous? Why did we never think of it? You ought to have thought of it, being the clever one. Oh, they knew you were the clever one, I didn't have to tell them. Sarah is intelligent, that's our Sarah!"

She sat down very erect on the bed.

"You've had too much to drink."

"I expect so. I expect so. Everyone was so kind. My dear, you don't know who your friends are, do you? And there was a man, rather a pet —"

"So long as there was a man," Sarah said.

Helen stopped swinging her legs and stared.

Sarah went on. "They were laughing at you. I suppose you didn't realise that, not being the clever one. You look absurd, all dolled up like that. Of course they were laughing. And your hair is coming down."

Helen's stare was prolonged. Suddenly her face grew very red, then crumpled, creasing her make-up like a relief map. She began to cry. Sarah undressed her without tenderness or embarrassment and put her to bed. When she herself was in bed she lay awake watching the moon riding across the window. She gave up all hope of sleep until rousing she realised that the moon had gone and the thin dawn light was at the window. She propped herself on her elbow, staring across at Helen's bed. It was empty. She rose and put her hands on the crumpled sheets; they were quite cold. She jerked her burberry off its hook, put on her shoes and went cautiously down the stairs, through the lounge which smelt of stale cigarette smoke, into the dining-room set for breakfast with tomorrow's marmalade pots. No sign anywhere of Helen. The catch of the French window was unfastened, she pushed it open and went into the garden, up and down the paths, empty, all empty. The curtained windows of the sleeping house filled her with lonely panic. She thought longingly of the telephone and strangled an insane impulse to ring George. She set off down the steep street. Papers blew about the little park. All the park seats were empty. The lighthouse, whose beam had already lost some of its virtue in the growing greyness, lit empty doorways, empty alleys, deserted streets. The air was sharp and lively. Seagulls, returning from night pastures, went over her head, crying. Passing a shop window whose blind was drawn she was startled by her reflection moving in it. No trace anywhere of Helen.

She reached the shore, stumbling over the fine pebbles and brittle seaweed to the strip of sand where the tide, already falling, left a dark stain all along its edge. The sea looked sluggish, like oil. There were no waves, only a sudden collapse of water, startingly unrhythmic.

Helen was on her hands and knees, a few yards out in the tide which lapped her shoulders. The exhausted beam of the lighthouse shone on her shoulders where the soaked nightdress had slipped down. She crawled forward, moaning, dipping her face in the water and lifting it, dipping it again, asking the sea to do for her what she needed.

"Helen!" She didn't move or turn. "Helen!"

Sarah waded out, calling. Helen had heard her and was plunging deeper into the water. Just before she reached her the lighthouse's beam was extinguished and the sun's cold ray lit points of fire in the faintly heaving sea.

Helen's forearm when at last she gripped it was heavy and solid with cold. "Let me go. Let me go."

They struggled in the water. "Stand up. Stand up." If she falls I will not have the strength to lift her. "Stand up." "Let me go."

At last she was upright, but with little strength left to stand. Sarah gripped her. Their bodies, balanced against each other in the rise and fall of the water, were joined and made separate by their breasts.

Helen stopped fighting and leaned against Sarah, weeping. "I tried! I tried!"

Somehow they made their way to the shore. Water ran from their clothing and Sarah's shoes sucked the pavement. Helen's feet were bare and cut. Cats returning from night prowling stared at them. All colours were still grey. An early lorry jolted past. The steep street rose up in front of them. "Not far now." A light flicked on behind a drawn blind. The soaked edges of Sarah's coat swung and hit her legs. Helen had begun to shake uncontrollably. "Hurry, hurry."

They turned in at the Hotel entrance. Helen sank down on a seat in the porch. The door was open. Sarah found James in the hall. He had been leaving shoes at bedroom doors and

172

wore a jacket over his pyjamas. Even in this undress he still looked the everlasting servant.

"Miss Vincent!"

"Mrs. Harris is ill, James."

"The doctor – will I ring for him?"

"No. No one. No one, James."

He came outside with her. When he saw Helen he took off his jacket and wrapped it round her before he gathered her against him. Her eyes were closed, her face grey, worn, old, hair plastered. It was a pity she could not have seen the look of inexpressible homage with which he took her to her room.

CHAPTER THIRTEEN

HERE, at the farther end of the cemetery, the hum of traffic on the main road sounded no louder than the bees who circulated among the open-throated flowers of the wreaths. Like Helen, Kitty had tried, but she had succeeded where Helen had failed. After she had taken the overdose of sleeping-tablets she lay in Hospital for a week before she died. An open verdict was returned at the inquest, and sympathy was expressed.

She was buried on a brilliant summer morning. It was the final week in August, sunlight already had a ripe autumnal quality, appropriate to the occasion. How can we bear to bury anyone in the restless dazzle of spring? From the fields beyond the cemetery rose the rusty double note of a corn-crake and on the other side Lough water danced. Probably the tiger aloft in his cage looked down on the knot of figures and noticed how the ladies kept together, neither straggling nor diffident, as if in this crisis there was some strength to be derived from the habit of the class-room.

There had been no Church service and they sang 'The Lord's my Shepherd' at the open grave, firmly, without the invitation of the minister and without any fuss. The Lord is my Shepherd and the twenty-third psalm is His sheep-dog, though the lusty Jewish King would have been surprised to find himself in the same flock as these gloved and saddened ladies who came to Kitty's funeral on the day when they should have gathered for their tea-party.

In school concerts and Church choirs they had been accustomed to singing together, and though their voices were not as fresh as they used to be they were rounded and composed. It was a relief, after the few words spoken when they were crowded elbow to elbow in the darkened house to be singing together in the open air. Sarah's contralto was true and steady though tears ran down her face. Florence and Enid slid easily into the descant. It was years since they had felt such unity of purpose, and in this sunlight it did not frighten them to realise that there would be other occasions like this one when each of them in turn would act as hostess to the others. They would still be afraid singly, but as a corporate exercise death was neither sad nor alarming.

Nor on this occasion were they embarrassed by being moved in each others' company. For most of them, brought up in Provincial religious homes, faith as they grew older had become an individual solitary relationship, shy, ingrown, a protest against the public emphasis on their Protestantism, against too loud Orange drums and the hysteria of spawning Mission Halls. They were products of their environment and generation who had retained the habit of faith as they had the habit of cleaning their teeth, both learnt in childhood, and recognised that these were private occupations. But death was an event where the presence of God the Father was justified.

George stood by himself, leaning towards the grave, as if before it closed there was still some kind of a chance. It was unacceptable that Kitty's unhappiness was over just because she had stopped breathing. He seemed to be fighting for a desperate final sincerity and had armed himself against the interruption of sympathy. There were some cousins of Kitty whom no one knew, up from the country for the funeral, since dying is a family affair. Maurice stood behind them, pompous and distressed, deputising for Joyce, whose baby was due in a few weeks. Florence had come with her distinguished husband, both outstandingly unobtrusive. But it was significant that he was beside Maurice and Florence had joined Addie who wore a feathered hat clamped round her ears, like something out of *Swan Lake* only in black, and twisted her gloves. Mary had come with two of her married daughters. They held hands as they sang. Sarah had motored from the seaside that morning. Helen, she told them, was still recovering from the severe chill she had caught during her stay at the Hotel. The flowers that had come from Helen's shop were conspicuously lavish and beautiful. She would be well enough for Sarah to bring her back to town in a day or two.

> 'Goodness and mercy all my life
> Shall surely follow me.'

This was difficult, for they did not think that they had followed poor unhappy Kitty – or at least she had not allowed them to catch up with her. They had not liked Kitty very much and didn't think she had liked them, and if in the closing verse they tottered on the edge between sincerity and sentiment it was because on this golden day sadness was unbearable, and the starkness of death must somehow be clothed.

The singing was over, earth fell on the coffin and from the Shore Road a factory horn intruded thinly. Their unity dissolved and they turned raggedly for the gate, leaving George to make what sense out of it he could.

Sarah inquired for Joyce and Maurice told her that she was as well as could be expected. This and his nervous manner irritated Sarah who said, "Oh, come now, Maurice. I'm sure she's a little better than that," and he gave her a reproachful look and drove off quickly in his car. Florence reminded them all of the urgency of her current Bazaar. One of Mary's daughters unexpectedly was crying. There must be another on the way; she should not have come.

Sarah took Addie back to Thronehill. She wanted very badly to speak to George who still had not moved from the graveside, but it was impossible. In any case the posse of cousins was closing in on him. She thought of him lying on the bed. "Pretty Kitty, pretty Kitty."

Addie kicked her shoes off and leant back in the car.

"'In my Father's house there are many mansions', one is thankful for that." She looked small and pinched. "I mock, I mock. What is it about being this age that makes us do it? I don't mean to, but I do it. Am I being honest or sour, I wish I knew. I expected by this time to have something more mature to say, but all I produce is a silly babble." She wept quietly, mopping her eyes with her gloves.

Sarah patted her knee self-consciously, keeping one eye on the traffic. "Are you all right, Addie?"

"Of course I'm all right."

"You haven't been having any more of your turns?"

"Dear Sarah, I love you. I am just a little exhausted with emotion and fury at being a provincial lady and not much more time even to be that. What do you suppose happened to us? Modesty and duty, what do you think we expected to get out of that little lot? There used to be something called nobility, too. You only hear about it nowadays in Church. And the emancipation of women going on all round us. Or was it the wars that queered our pitch? Do you remember Miss Alison at school – perpetually in rose beige and we suspected she used a lipstick. 'Live boldly and strongly, girls.' I used to look at her and wonder if she managed it."

Sarah said, "I think we've done pretty well, all things considered. We have established a type. Society doesn't recognise a type unless it has some significance."

"And we have our moments of glory. This morning we were magnificent and indestructible – did you feel that? Now back to the old routine. Keep interested, that's what the Sunday paper psychologists are always saying. Be alive to what goes on around you. I try, I try. I read articles on marriage guidance and homosexuality and frigidity, and I try to get used to things like sexual intercourse cropping up in the eight o'clock news, but one feels there must be other equally rewarding topics."

Sarah changed the subject. "How is Gerald? Has he been feeling better while we've been away?"

Addie cried, "I don't know, and frankly at this moment I don't care," and she wept again, more noisily.

Presently she pulled herself together. "What happened to Helen?"

"I told you. She caught a bad chill. There was a thunderstorm and she got drenched."

"Thunder? We didn't have any here. But we are all going to pieces now, one way and another. We will have arthritis and coronaries and break our hips and have less and less hair to drape round our Deaf-Aids. Some of us will carry on to a sprightly sixty-five or seventy, and a few of us may strike eighty and have to decide who we are going to be a burden to. Not that my mother was a burden, you mustn't think that. Never. Not once."

"Addie, I wish you weren't so low."

"I am indulging myself. There is nothing so comfortable as black despair. Poor George, didn't you feel sorry for him? I didn't think I could, but it is the first time I've seen him looking unsuccessful. It's always so different from what you expect it to be, isn't it?"

Sarah turned in at the gate.

Addie asked, "What will Helen do now, that's what I would like to know. Or is that something I'm not supposed to ask?"

Sarah drew up and switched the engine off. "Helen? She's talking of giving up the shop and going to live in London."

Addie stared. "London?"

"She's finding the work at the shop too much for her."

"You mean —?"

"Helen has plenty of friends in London."

Addie's stare turned to a look of genuine concern. "Oh, my poor Sarah," she said and went up the steps, calling urgently for Gerald before she had reached the door.

The extraordinary thing is that I didn't need Addie's pity

at all. It was over, that was all. I suppose it had lasted forty-five years and it was over. What had happened wasn't painful or difficult, it wasn't anything that needed any effort or argument, it didn't even call for any regret. I made no conscious decision, nor did I need to justify any. It was simply an ending.

Of course I was tired, tired to the bone. At first I thought that what I felt was simply due to tiredness, to the shock and being up all night with Helen. But it was more than that.

I left her sleeping when I went down to breakfast the next morning. I thought it better to go, though I felt dizzy with fatigue and everything was an effort. I noticed that there were no patches of sea-water on the stairs or on the tiles in the hall. I suppose James had seen to that.

"Mrs. Harris has caught a slight chill," I told him, "she will be staying in her room for a few days." And he agreed that the weather could be tricky at this time of the year.

When he came to tell me Mr. Pedlow was on the telephone asking to speak to Mrs. Harris I said I would take the call. I wondered what I should say to George, but felt too exhausted to believe that it mattered very much one way or another. He gave me no time to say anything, but told me about Kitty. He had been at the Hospital with her all night; they believed that she had a chance.

I suppose I didn't answer because he said, "Are you there, Sarah?" and his voice sounded unreal and a long way off. I made an effort and asked if he would like me to tell Helen, and he said, "Would you?" and I put the receiver on and went upstairs.

Helen was awake. Her face was pink after sleeping, and her hair had dried in little curls on her forehead. I noticed these things, though they were no more to me than facts. "You have caught a chill and you are spending the day in your room," I told her, and she put out a hand towards me and said, "Dearest Sarah, you saved my life."

I didn't come any closer so that her hand fell into space. I said, "I'm glad you're grateful. I wondered." Then I told her about George's phone call and about Kitty.

She was fairly ill for a few days. She didn't speak very much, or eat the food they sent – everyone in the Hotel was kind and concerned for her – and I don't think she slept much either though I didn't stay awake to find out. We lived entirely separate and independent lives in the same room. I wondered about George and Kitty and I prayed for them, not specifically because there didn't seem to me to be any solution, but asking that God's will should be done, which was a passive and useless thing to do, I suppose, since obviously God needed no prompting from me. And I slept and did cross-words and rested my leg.

It was very peaceful. In a sense it was like being let out of prison, not wondering whether Helen was happy or unhappy, not feeling any reaction to her moods or any responsibility for her or them, not waiting for her to speak, not being her audience and mirror any more. I could almost have loved her for having let me go.

On Friday I read the notice of Kitty's death in the paper and I showed it to Helen. That evening she said suddenly, "What shall I do, Sarah?"

I asked if she had seen Hubert when she was in London, and she told me she had lunched with him.

She gave me a guarded glance and I knew she wanted me to say the words for her instead of having to say them herself. Do this last thing for me, Sarah. So I said, "I expect he wants you to go back to him, doesn't he?" and she said he did.

"I believe it mightn't be a bad idea."

Her face was already animated. "Do you really think so?"

"Yes." It was like ruling a line across the bottom of an exercise.

I rang up the Hotel when I got back to the flat after Kitty's funeral and they told me Helen had had a restful day, so I decided not to go down until the morning and they said they would tell her. This was a thing I could not have done a week ago, and it filled me with quiet elation to be able to. There were letters at the flat for me and I went through them. An English Anthology wanted to print one of my verses. The beast, whom I hadn't seen for a long time, woke up, but when he found there was no fee involved he grumbled that he couldn't go on polishing his scales on prestige for ever. There was a letter from a literary society in the city asking me to address them. I told the beast and he said, "And you can guess from the lady who proposes the vote of thanks which poem of yours she has read." There was a small formal note from George, written in reply to my small formal note. He thanked me for all the kindness I had shown to Kitty. He said he thought she had relied on me more than on anyone else. I wondered if he included himself, and if so whether it cost him anything to tell me this.

I saw Addie cycling down the drive briskly, wearing a red scarf. I was glad she had recovered her high spirits. Her bell trilled at the gate. Justin and Felicity were lying in each others' arms in the long grass below the trees. The baby, who was sitting up now, watched them gravely from his pram. Felicity had been hanging out washing and she still wore the little scarlet stomacher that held her pegs. Justin put his hands under it, embracing her belly. She smiled and they rolled over, laughing and kissing. This was too much for the solemn child who began to roar. Justin went into the house and Felicity rocked the pram.

I decided to go and ask Gerald how he was, I hadn't seen him since I'd got back. He switched off the television manfully and took his fingers from the cat's nape.

"And where's Addie off to?" I asked him. "I saw her skimming down the drive like a swallow."

"They were to have her results today."

"Results?"

"At the Hospital – the X-ray."

"X-ray? She didn't tell me."

"A lot of nonsense, so Addie said. It was the doctor, he seemed to think it should be done."

CHAPTER FOURTEEN

"'STOP, my postilion has been struck by lightning,'" Addie giggled. "One never knows, does one?"

"How are you, Addie?"

"According to nurse I am remarkably bright." Addie's sharp-featured face looked less live than the gleaming pillow it lay against. 'Remarkably bright considering,' the nurse had said to Sarah as she conveyed her through corridors to Addie's room. "Such a pleasant girl, Sarah, did you notice her? Just like Phoebe West, do you remember Phoebe? She did Tony Lumpkin, you must remember. And her chilblains used to burst every year. Didn't you think she was like Phoebe?"

"I didn't notice," Sarah said. She had noticed nothing, concerned only for Addie, wondering what she could find to say. She need not have worried, for there was behind the evidence of pain a kind of excited triumph in Addie's eyes.

"The surgeon is such a nice man," Addie said, "exactly right."

"When is it to be? Have they said?"

"On Friday – what he calls 'taking a look round', such a genteel way to put it, don't you think?"

"Addie, is there anything I can do? What about Gerald? I could look after him."

"That is sweet of you, but he's going to his sister. One feels happier making a nuisance of oneself with relations, don't you think? Perhaps you'd pop into the flat sometimes, and keep an eye."

"I will, I will."

"Everyone has been so kind," Addie beamed, "you can't imagine. Fruit from dear Mary, the glossiest of magazines from Florence, and these flowers from Helen, like something out of the Arabian Nights. When does Helen leave?"

"I'm taking her to the airport this evening."

"My poor Sarah, no wonder you look dreary."

"That is no remark from a patient to a visitor," Sarah scolded.

Addie's hand slid under the pillow and drew out an envelope. "Read that, Sarah. It came this morning."

Sarah hesitated.

"Go on, read it."

She lay back, breathing sharply but her eyes were dwellings of contentment. Sarah read the cable. Five lines of love. He would think of her all the time. She must think of him. He was flying back to Ireland on Saturday.

"On Saturday, he'll be here."

Sarah handed back the envelope. The nurse appeared at the door. "I think you shouldn't stay much longer, Miss Vincent. Mrs. Pratt tires easily."

"Very exhausting, lying in bed," Addie commented.

Sarah said, "I can see you are going to be impossible, Addie."

"I hope so, I hope so," Addie said briskly, but there was a hint of panic in her eyes.

"Please Miss Vincent —"

"How the girl creates," Addie grumbled contentedly. "But Gerald is coming this evening."

Sarah said good-bye and stumbled into the corridor behind the starched apron strings, feeling much more shaken than the patient she had left and sat in the car for a while before she felt able to drive back to Thronehill. She passed George's parked car at the gate without identifying it, and found him with Helen when she went into the flat.

"I'm sorry," she said, "I didn't know —"

"Don't go away Sarah – come in."

She had not seen George since Kitty's funeral three weeks ago. Nor indeed had she seen very much of Helen since her return from the Hotel, just enough to notice with sad relief the zest with which Helen was making her preparations to leave. "My dear, so much to do, a hundred things to think about." Dress-boxes arrived by every delivery, there were farewell parties in the flat below, long telephone conversations. Whether to admire her for her courage or criticise her for the success of her self-deception it was difficult to say. The girls at the shop made her a presentation. There was no trace of her illness, she went about with starry-eyed energy. "My dear, I am doing the right thing." Her friends assured her that she was. "I'm so glad you think so."

"George is just leaving," Helen said, "no need to run away. It was sweet of you to come, George."

They were glad to see her. It dawned on Sarah that her interruption had been providential. They needed an audience to make their adieux. It had been the relationship and not each other with which they had been in love. Since Kitty's death nothing could grow. She watched them, with the ardour and formality of ballet-dancers taking farewell of each other.

"Good-bye, my dear."

"Good-bye, Helen. And you know that I wish you all the luck there is."

"I know. I know."

The kiss which could have been difficult became in front of Sarah an expertly satisfying performance. George went away.

Driving to the airport Helen said unexpectedly, "I know you think I'm shallow, Sarah." And when Sarah didn't answer, "I hope this is going to work."

"It will, it will. What was Hubert like?"

"Very sweet. But Sarah —"

"What?"

"He was an old gentleman. I suppose I should have known, should I?"

Someone had sent flowers to Helen at the airport. She held

185

them against her as if to warm herself. "Lovely! Aren't people kind?" Passengers and officials glanced in her direction with interest. When the flight was announced she turned to Sarah pushing the flowers into her hands. "Take these. Good-bye, Sarah."

"Good-bye."

Cheeks touched, fingers tangled, and it was over. She watched Helen walking out to the plane, saw her turn, raise her hand, mount the steps. How easily it happens at the end. That is all. It is over. Go home now.

She had thought her home-coming would be quiet, too quiet, but as she switched off her engine she heard the baby's full-throated yell. Justin, carrying the child clumsily, came from the stable-flat. He looked ill-tempered and tired.

"What are the floral decorations in aid of?" he said, "and what am I going to do with this little lot? He's been carrying on like this for three-quarters of an hour."

"Where is his mother?"

"What did you say?"

They bellowed at each other across the red-faced screaming child.

"His Mother!"

"Gone to the Clinic."

"I expect he's missing her."

"I expect so. Look – isn't there anything you can do?"

"Me?"

"You must have some idea what to do with a baby," Justin accused.

She pointed out, "You are his father, and you are likely to have a good deal more to do with him in the future."

He pushed out a sulky lip. "I dare say, but what shall I do at the present moment?"

"If I were you I should take him to the Zoo."

"Where?"

"The Zoo. Animals and things."

"Maybe you're right." He lashed the unwilling child

186

into the pram. "Come on, see nice giraffes, lions, growly bears."

They set off noisily down the drive. Sarah went into the house. It was very quiet. No one in the house except herself. Helen's door lay open. Empty, all empty.

There were, as usual, papers to correct. The Senior girls competing for the Literature medal. Elizabeth was the favourite. A foregone conclusion. Sarah scanned her paper hopefully. A good student, more mature than most in her judgements, an interesting girl. But – oh, how stupid, how incredibly careless! She had forgotten to answer a question from Section 4. What could one do? No matter how brilliant her other answers, what could one do? She need only have attempted it.

The bell rang and she looked out of the window and saw the top of Maurice's head. "Maurice, what is it?"

"I must come up. Please let me come up."

"The key's in the lock, then," she said gracelessly.

He arrived, breathless, in a few minutes. "I am hiding from dear Mary," he panted, "you must give me shelter."

"What do you mean?"

"Joyce is in labour."

"Poor Maurice, poor Maurice. And what has Mary done?"

"She has promised Joyce to 'see me through,' whatever that means. I think she intends giving me a detailed report of what ought to be happening every five minutes if everything goes according to plan. But, oh my God, what a plan! I've been dodging Mary all day. I am afraid to go home."

"When did it start?"

"Hours and hours ago – in the middle of last night, actually. She's in Hospital."

"Then you should be there too. It could happen any time now."

Maurice sat down, holding his head and moaning gently. She urged, "You should, you know."

"In a minute. In a minute. Let me stay a little while."
He calmed and lit a cigarette, blew out smoke, relaxed and
eased his shoulders into the back of his chair. "Sarah, look
at the old monkey puzzle. I wonder how old that tree is.
Part of our childhood. We used to make dragons out of
it when the evening sun was behind it like that, do you
remember?"

"No."

"Sarah, you must!"

"You should be at the Hospital."

He looked grieved and said, "You're sending me away."

"Yes."

"I don't know how you can."

"I can because your child is going to be born any time now
and you ought to be there."

He got up heavily, stabbing out his cigarette. She put a
hand on his sleeve and said, "It will be all right, Maurice. It
will."

He said, "I'm afraid, Sarah. It could happen twice."

"I don't think it will."

"It was Rose's child I wanted."

"Rose is dead and Joyce is alive and your child is being
born."

He dropped his head. "I suppose I'd better go, then."

She steered him towards the door. "Yes. Yes. And give
Joyce my love. And ring me up tonight, if you remember."

"I will. I will."

She heard him going downstairs heavily, but with more
purpose than he had climbed a few minutes before. The house
when he had left it seemed to ring with silence. The sun going
down behind the monkey puzzle made a procession of magnificent dragons.

I shall telephone someone, that's what I'll do. Who is there?
Someone I know well but not too well, so that it will be easy
afterwards to extricate myself. I will think of someone. I must
talk, must dabble in friendship before I am content again

188

with my own company. I am tired and confused, too much has happened. Too many good-byes.

It was a silly game, she had no appetite for it. Even her voice in the empty house – "Such ages since I'd heard anything of you – couldn't we have lunch some time?" – would be startling and unreal. Panic crept round the perimeter of her mind.

She would go now and talk to Mama who would be lying in bed, prepared for the night, quiet and calm and orderly, with her book, her glass of water, her bottle of pills. They would find something to say to each other. Or to Papa. Perhaps he was seated comfortably in front of the last of the fire, fondling the glass that held his bedtime whisky, turning it round, seeing the flames strike points of light in it, Papa peaceful and omnipotent, an exorcist of terrors.

She went downstairs quickly, first to Mama's room, then to the drawing-room. They were empty, dark, quiet. No one. No one. Reality blazed on her confused mind. They are dead. They will not be here any more. They are all dead. I will not see them again or hear them. I will never see them again. They are dead.

Back then to her own room and by an exercise of discipline back to the examination papers and the problem of Elizabeth. The evening sky drew her eyes again to the window and she saw Justin coming back with a tired and peaceful baby. Felicity came back. The light in their flat burned peacefully. Gerald was still at the Hospital. Helen would be in London by this time.

It was only sufficiently light for her to recognise George when he came. He was walking quickly. When he reached the lowest step he halted and stared up in the direction of her window. There was an air of necessity about him. No flower in his lapel, but his buttonhole looked as if with a little warmth it might sometime bud again. A thin and neglected beast ran at his heels. It was honest of him, she thought, to have brought his beast.

She withdrew into the room trembling, and sat at her desk. It is absurd. I cannot meet him. I will not let him come. This is something I refuse to confront. Now that Kitty is dead and Helen has gone away we have nothing to say to each other, nothing from which to build a relationship. We do not speak the same language; we are hardly the same species.

She began to gather up the papers on her desk with clumsy confused fingers. Then she remembered Elizabeth, and how even a promising candidate who does not attempt to answer a question from every section will fail to satisfy the examiners. Laughter, like brass bands, filled her, but her face was grave as she laid the papers on the desk again and stood up, and turned to the door, waiting for him to come.